THE FATHER BROWN READER
Stories from Chesterton

Adapted by Nancy Carpentier Brown
with Rose Decaen

Illustrated by Ted Schluenderfritz

ISBN: 978-0-9766386-7-4

Text adapted by Nancy Carpentier Brown with Rose Decaen
Illustrations and book design by Ted Schluenderfritz

Hillside Education
475 Bidwell Hill Road
Lake Ariel, PA 18436

www.hillsideeducation.com

FOR MIKE,

My one and only love,
You are wonderful.

PREFACE

This book contains adapted versions of some of Chesterton's Father Brown mysteries. The Father Brown stories are amazing mysteries that children of all ages can enjoy. We have adapted them in our efforts to make Chesterton's works available to a wider audience. If you enjoy reading these adaptations, we recommend that someday you read the original books!

Book One

THE BLUE CROSS

by G. K. Chesterton

THE BLUE CROSS

CHAPTER ONE
Valentin and Flambeau

A silver dawn graced the London sky as a boat landed in the glittering harbor at Harwich. People exited the ferry like a swarm of flies, moving in and among each other and hurrying in different directions. Among the confusion was a man who easily could have gone unnoticed—and he certainly wished to be inconspicuous. There was nothing special about him, except perhaps, the serious look on his face which was at odds with his holiday clothing: a pale gray jacket and a silver straw hat. His face was thin, his skin was dark, and he had a narrow black beard. Like many other men on holiday, he carried an elegant walking cane. There was nothing to indicate that under his jacket was a loaded revolver, that in his pocket was a police identification card, or that under his hat was one of the best brains, one of the most powerful intellects, in all of Europe. This was Valentin himself, the head of the Paris police, the most famous investigator in the world. He had just arrived in London to make the greatest arrest of the century.

For Flambeau, the notorious criminal, was in England. The police of three countries had tracked him from city to city across Europe, and now they had guessed that he would take advantage of the confusion and crowds attending the Eucharistic Congress in London.[1] Probably, he would pretend to be some minor clerk or parish priest, but no one knew that for certain; nobody could be certain about Flambeau.

For months now, Europe had been quiet. After robberies and crimes had been committed in all directions by Flambeau—when the papers had news of his great (I mean his awful) accomplishments almost daily—suddenly, it was quiet. And the quiet was disturbing to the police chief. He knew that when Flambeau was quiet, something was going to happen.

In all of Europe, this was one criminal whom no one could capture; one who had escaped from every impossible situation and slipped out of the consequences of one extraordinary crime after another. He was a man of gigantic proportions and bodily daring. It is due to him to say that his fantastic physical strength was generally not used to harm others; his real crimes were those of ingenious and wholesale robbery. Each of his thefts was almost a new sin and would make a story by itself. It is he who ran the great Tyrolean Dairy Company in London, with no dairies, no cows, no carts, no milk, but with some thousand subscribers. These he served by the simple operation of moving the little milk cans outside people's doors to the doors of his own customers. It is said that he once repainted all the numbers in a street in the dead of night merely to divert one traveler into a trap. He once invented a portable mailbox, which he occasionally set up on a street corner, on the chance that some stranger might be mailing money. He went about Europe, traveling in every sort of disguise. Once, he dressed up as an old lady, all bent over, with a long old dress and a cane. He had been a chef, a blind beggar on the street, a juggler, a policeman, and even a nun. There seemed to be no end of characters that Flambeau could play. And in each case, he was able to get away with some world-class theft. Lastly, he was known to be a startling acrobat; despite his huge figure, he could leap like a grasshopper and melt into the treetops like a monkey. Hence the great Valentin, when he set out to find Flambeau, was perfectly aware that his adventures would not end when he had found him.

And yet, even though Flambeau was a master of disguise, he could not hide one thing: his height. Flambeau was six feet, four inches tall. All of this was rattling around in Valentin's head as he walked among the crowds on holiday. How, he wondered, could he begin to find Flambeau?

CHAPTER TWO
A Small Priest, Flambeau, Valentin, and London

Since Valentin was searching London for someone with extraordinary height, if his eye caught a tall apple-woman, a tall soldier, even a tall duchess, he might have arrested them on the spot. But about the people on the boat, he was already convinced that there were no tall persons who disembarked. About the six people who transferred from the boat to the train as he did, he was equally certain. There was a short railway official, three fairly short farmers coming in to sell the produce from their gardens, one very short widow lady, and a very short Roman Catholic priest. When it came to the last, Valentin almost laughed to himself. The little priest had a face as round and dull as a dumpling, with eyes as empty as the sea. He had several brown paper parcels, which continuously seemed to be falling out of his grasp.

Valentin thought the Eucharistic Congress must have drawn all of the priests, even the slow and unqualified, out of their quiet little rectories, like moles drawn out of their underground homes. Valentin himself was a certified skeptic, and had no love for priests. But he could feel sorry for them, and this one certainly could draw the pity of the famous inspector. The priest had a large, shabby umbrella, which kept falling to the floor. He couldn't seem to figure out which was the right end of his return ticket.

During the trip, the priest kept mentioning in all simplicity that he had to be very careful, because he carried a "pretty cross," of "real silver with blue stones" in one of his brown paper parcels. His quaint way of speaking continuously amused the Frenchman till the priest arrived (somehow) at Tottenham with all his parcels and came back for his umbrella. When he did the last, Valentin even had the good nature to warn him not to take care of the silver by telling everybody about it. But to whomever he talked, Valentin kept an eye open for someone else; he looked out steadily for anyone, rich or poor, male or female, who was well up to six feet tall.

Valentin left the platform and checked in with Scotland Yard.[2]

He wanted to let them know that he had trailed Flambeau this far (to London) and that he might need their help, if by chance he could discover what it was that Flambeau was after this time. Then, he went for a walk on the streets of London. He was strolling along casually, still on the alert for tall citizens, when, as he gazed along the street, a restaurant caught his eye.

Like many restaurants one might see along the street, flowers were arranged carefully at the front door and the windows all had lemon yellow and white blinds. But what really drew Valentin's eye was that when one looked at all the buildings on this street, one could see that this particular restaurant was much higher than the rest of the buildings. In fact, one had to ascend quite a steep set of stairs just to get up to this restaurant.

Now, Aristide Valentin was a world famous inspector for a reason. He had an ability to just "know" when something was different, or something was out of place. He looked at the restaurant, and somehow, his detective soul could smell that something was possible there. You see, Valentin knew that the most incredible thing about miracles is that they happen. A few clouds in heaven do come together into the staring shape of one human eye. A tree does stand up in the landscape of a doubtful journey in the exact and elaborate shape of a question mark. And Valentin's experience taught him to search for and follow such unusual coincidences and hunches. When he could not follow a logical train of thought, he coldly and carefully followed the train of the unreasonable. And so, he knew he had to go to that restaurant. There was something in that high flight of stairs, something in the quaintness of the restaurant, that told Valentin, "Enter here." So he did.

CHAPTER THREE
At the Restaurant

*V*alentin walked up the steps, and sat down at a table near the window of the restaurant. He ordered a cup of black coffee. It was mid-morning, and Valentin could smell food, the aroma was drifting over from the kitchen. He realized that he had missed his breakfast, so he summoned the waiter and added a poached egg to his order. He spooned out some sugar into his coffee, and sat there stirring, all the while thinking about Flambeau. He was remembering how Flambeau had escaped in the past. Once, he escaped because he had a nail clipper, and once, by setting a house on fire. Once he escaped by having to pay for a stamp on a letter he was mailing, and once by getting people to look through a telescope at a comet. Valentin thought his detective's brain was as good as the criminal's brain, and that was true. But he also realized his disadvantage. Flambeau could be creative, and he, Valentin, could only follow after and approve or disapprove Flambeau's methods. He lifted his cup to his lips slowly, and then put it down again very quickly. He had put salt in it.

He looked at the sugar bowl. He was certain that it was a sugar bowl. He wondered why they should keep salt in it. He looked to see what other containers were on his table. He also had two saltshakers on his table, both quite full. He wondered now what was in the saltshakers. He tasted it; it was sugar.

Then, he looked around the restaurant with new eyes, to see if there were any other traces of that artist's hand, the one who would put sugar in saltshakers and salt in sugar bowls. Except for an odd splash of dark fluid on one of the white walls, the whole place appeared neat, cheerful, and ordinary. He called for his waiter.

The waiter approached the table, and the detective asked him to taste the sugar and see if it was up to the high reputation of the restaurant. The waiter, who had been rather sleepy this morning, suddenly woke up, as he tasted the "sugar."

"Do you play this kind of practical joke on your customers every morning?" asked Valentin. "Does changing the salt and sugar never fail to amuse you?"

The waiter stammered, and reassured the detective that this restaurant would never play such a joke, that it was a most unusual mistake. The waiter picked up the sugar bowl, looked at it; he picked up the saltshaker and looked at that, and his face showed that he was absolutely bewildered. At last, he excused himself, hurried away, and returned a few seconds later with the owner of the restaurant. The owner also examined the sugar bowl and the saltshaker, and now the owner looked bewildered.

Suddenly, the waiter began to speak in a rush of words.

"I zink," he stuttered eagerly, "I zink it is zoze two clergymen."

"What two clergymen?"

"The two clergymen," said the waiter, "that threw the soup at the wall."

"Threw soup at the wall?" repeated Valentin, wondering if this was some peculiar Italian metaphor.

"Yes, yes," said the waiter excitedly, and pointed at the dark splash on the white paper, "threw it over there on the wall."

Valentin looked at the waiter, then at the owner, hoping for more of an explanation.

"Yes, sir," the owner said, "it is true, though I don't suppose it has anything to do with the sugar and the salt. Well, two priests came in here and had soup very early in the morning. They were both quiet and seemed respectable. One of them paid the bill and went out; the other, who seemed a slower person, was some minutes longer getting all his packages and things together. But, at last, he went. Only, the instant before he stepped into the street, he picked up his bowl of soup, which he had only half emptied, and threw the soup slap against the wall. The waiter and I were in the back room when it happened, and we rushed out to find the wall splashed and the dining room empty. I don't have any idea why he did it, but I thought it was a display of confounded cheek; and I tried to catch the men in the street. They were too far off though. I only noticed that they went round the next corner to Carstairs Street."

The detective was on his feet in an instant, hat settled and walking stick in hand. He had already decided in the universal darkness of his mind that he could only follow the first odd finger that pointed; and this finger was odd enough. Paying his bill and clashing the glass doors behind him, he was soon swinging round into the street looking for anything that might be the next clue.

CHAPTER FOUR
On the Street

*H*is eyes were sharp as he scanned the scene in front of him. Was there anything out of place? Was there anything to notice that might help him in his search?

As he ran, something peculiar in a shop-front went by him like a mere flash; so, he went back to look at it. The shop had fruits and vegetables in front of it, set out in the open air and plainly marked with prices and names of the items for sale. One of the most noticeable was a box of oranges and next to it a box of nuts. On the heap of nuts lay a scrap of cardboard, on which was written in bold, blue chalk, "Best tangerine oranges, two a penny." On the oranges was the equally clear and exact description, "Finest Brazilian nuts, $4 a pound." Valentin looked at the two signs, and thought that he had seen this brand of humor before, and that it had been just recently.

He called out to the fruit merchant, who was looking rather angrily up and down the street, and asked him about the switched sign cards. The fruit merchant said nothing, but sharply put each sign in its proper place. The detective, leaning elegantly on his walking cane, continued to examine the shop carefully. At last he said, "Please excuse me, my good sir, I would just like to ask you a question, if I may be so bold."

The shopkeeper regarded the detective with an eye

of menace, but Valentin continued as lightly as he could, swinging his cane casually, "Why," he asked, "why are two signs placed incorrectly in the fruit shop this morning? Or, if I may continue to be bold, is there any connection between the switched signs and two priests, one tall and the other short?"

The eyes of the fruit man stood out of his head like a snail's, and he almost attacked our detective, so upset was he about the recent events that had occurred at his fruit stand. At last, he stammered angrily: "I don't know what you 'ave to do with it, but if you're one of their friends, you can tell 'em for me that I'll knock their silly 'eads off, priests or no priests, if they upset my apples ever again."

"Indeed?" asked the detective with great sympathy, "Did they upset your apples?"

"One of 'em did," said the upset shopman, "rolled 'em all over the street. I'd 'ave caught him, too, but for havin' to pick 'em up."

"Which way did the priests go?" asked Valentin.

"Up that second road on the left-hand side, and then across the square," said the other promptly.

"Thanks," replied Valentin, and vanished like a fairy. On the other side of the square, he found a policeman, and said: "This is urgent, officer, have you seen two priests?"

The policeman began to chuckle, "I 'ave, sir, and if you ask me, one of them must have been drunk. He stood in the middle of the road, quite bewildered, and—"

"Which way did they go?" snapped Valentin.

"They took one of them yellow buses over there," answered the man, "one of the buses that goes to Hampstead."

Valentin showed the policeman his official identification card and said very quickly: "Call up two of your men to come with me in pursuit," and he crossed the road with such contagious energy that the larger policeman was moved to almost agile obedience. In a minute and a half an inspector and a plainclothes officer joined the French detective.

"Well, sir," began the English detective, with a sense of his own importance, "and what may—"

Valentin pointed suddenly with his cane, "I'll tell you on the bus," he said, and was darting and dodging across the tangle of traffic. When all three sat panting on the seats of the yellow bus, the London inspector said: "We could go four times faster in a taxi."

"Quite true," replied their leader, "if we had any idea at all of where we are going."

"Well, where are you going?" asked the other, staring.

Valentin frowned as he gazed out the window, then he said: "If you know what a man's doing, you get in

17

front of him. But if you want to guess what he's doing, then you better keep behind him. Stray when he strays; stop when he stops; and travel as slowly as he. Then you may see what he saw and may act as he acted. All we can do is to keep our eyes peeled for a strange thing."

"What sort of strange thing do you mean?" asked the inspector.

"Any sort of strange thing," answered Valentin, and then he sat back in his seat, and sunk into an obstinate silence.

CHAPTER FIVE

The Strange Thing is Noticed

*T*he bus crawled along up the northern roads for what seemed like hours on end. The great detective would not explain further, and per-haps his assistants felt a silent and growing doubt about the errand. Perhaps they also felt a growing need for lunch, as the hours had crept along, long past the normal lunchtime, and the long roads of the northern areas of London seemed endless. In fact, London died away in draggled taverns and dreary scrubs, and then was born again in blazing high streets and blatant hotels. It was like passing through several vulgar cities all just touching each other. But though the winter twilight was already threatening the road ahead of them, the Parisian detec-tive still sat watchful, eyeing the frontage of the streets that slid by on either side. By the time they had left Camden Town behind, the policemen were nearly asleep; at least they seemed to be, for they gave some-thing of a jump as Valentin leapt erect, struck a hand on each man's shoulder, and shouted to the driver to stop.

The two officers tumbled down the steps of the bus into the road without realizing why they had been awakened and disturbed. They looked around with wonder, and found Valentin triumphantly pointing his walking cane toward a window on the left side of the road. It was a large window that belonged to a restau-rant at the front of a spacious and elegant hotel. The window, like all the rest along the frontage of the hotel, was of frosted and figured glass. But, in the middle of it was a big, black smash, like a star in the ice.

"Our clue! At last," cried Valentin, waving his cane, "the place with the broken window."

"What clue? What window?" asked the higher-ranking inspector. "Why, what proof is there that this has anything to do with them?"

Valentin almost broke his cane with rage.

"Proof! The man is looking for proof! Of course, there's a good chance that this has nothing to do with them! But what else is there? We must follow this one wild possibility, or else we might as well just go home." He banged his way into the restaurant, followed by his companions. They were soon seated for a late lunch at a little table, and they looked at the star of smashed glass from the inside. Not that it provided any information to them, as yet.

"Got your window broken, I see," said Valentin to the waiter as he paid the bill.

"Yes sir," answered the waiter, bending busily over the change, to which Valentin silently added a huge tip. The waiter straightened himself up and was now a little more talkative.

"Ah, yes, sir," he said, "a very odd thing, that, sir."

"Indeed? Tell us about it," said the detective with a careless curiosity.

"Well, two gents in black came in," said the waiter, "two of those foreign priests that are all walking around. They had a small and quiet little lunch, and one of them paid for it and went out. The other one, the little one, was just going out to join him when I looked at my change again and found he'd paid me more than three times too much. 'Here,' I says to the chap who was nearly out the door, 'you've paid too much.' 'Oh,' he says, very cool, 'have we?' 'Yes,' I says, and I picked up the bill to show him. Then came the real surprise."

"What do you mean?" asked the famous detective.

"Well, I'd have sworn that I'd written four dollars and fifteen cents on that bill. But now I saw that I'd put down fourteen dollars and fifteen cents, as plain as day."

"Well," cried Valentin, slowly rising from the table, but keeping his eyes intently on the waiter, "what then?"

"The priest at the door he says very calmly, 'Sorry to confuse your accounts, but it'll pay for the window.' 'What window?' I says. 'The one I'm going to break,' he says, and smashed that blessed pane with his umbrella."

All three of the men at the table were now standing, and expressing their amazement. "Are we after escaped lunatics?" the police inspector muttered under his breath.

The waiter went on with some relish for the ridiculous story. "I was so knocked silly for a second, I couldn't do anything. The man marched out of the place and joined his friend just round the corner. Then they went so quick up Bullock Street that I couldn't catch them, though I ran like mad to do it."

"Bullock Street," said the detective, and shot up that street as quickly as the strange couple he pursued.

CHAPTER SIX
The Bakery

*T*he detective and his two police companions ran down the road, through a dark alley, and up darkened streets. Dusk was deepening, and the policemen weren't sure which direction they were actually going. The inspector, however, was pretty sure they were heading towards Hampstead Heath, a large open park to the north. Suddenly, there was one window which was lit. In all the darkness that they had passed down that street, this window stood out. Valentin stopped for a second in front of the lit window, and saw that it was a bakery and candy shop. After hesitating for just a moment, he went in, and stood among the baked sweets. There was a selection of candies, and Valentin looked at the chocolates. He selected a dozen chocolate cigars, which he purchased to give himself a chance to talk with the owner. He need not have taken such pains, though.

An elderly young woman working in the shop looked at Valentin as if he were any other customer who came into the store that day, until she noticed the two policemen who followed him in the door. Then she suddenly looked alert, and seemed more awake.

"Oh," she said, "if you've come about that parcel, I've sent it off already."

"Parcel!" repeated Valentin, and it was his turn to look alert.

"I mean the parcel the gentleman left—the priest gentleman."

"For goodness sake," said Valentin, leaning forward with his first real sign of eagerness, "tell us what exactly happened."

"Well," said the woman a little doubtfully, "the two priests came in about a half hour ago and bought some peppermints and talked a bit, and then went off towards the Heath. But a second later, one of them ran back in and says, 'Have I left a parcel?' Well, I looked everywhere and couldn't see one; so he says, 'Never mind; but if it should turn up, please mail it to this address,' and he left me the address and a bit of money for my trouble. And sure enough, though I thought I'd looked everywhere, I found he'd left a brown paper parcel, so I mailed it to the place he said. I can't remember the address now; it was somewhere in Westminster. But as the thing seemed so important, I thought the police had come about it."

"So they have," said Valentin shortly. "Is Hampstead Heath near here?"

"Straight ahead there for fifteen minutes," said the woman, "and you'll come right out in the open." Valentin sprang out of the shop and began to run. The other detectives followed him at a trot.

The street they threaded was so narrow and shut in by shadows that when they came out unexpectedly into the open they were startled to find the evening still so light and clear. A perfect dome of peacock green sank into gold amid the blackening trees and the dark violet distances. The glowing green tint was just deep enough to pick out in points of crystal one or two stars. All that was left of the daylight lay in a golden glitter across the edge of Hampstead Heath. Even though the day was late, there were still people lingering in the park. A few couples sat shapelessly on benches; and here and there a distant girl still shrieked on one of the swings. The sky deepened and darkened, but as Valentin scanned the park with his sharpest eyes, he finally found the thing he sought.

Among the black and breaking groups in that distance, one was especially black and did not break up—a group of two priestly figures. Though they seemed small as insects, Valentine could see that one of them was much smaller than the other. While the taller had a stoop and a casual manner, he could see that the man was well over six feet tall. Valentin walked briskly forward with his teeth clenched and whirling his stick impatiently, shortening the distance between himself and the two priests. As he got closer, he began to understand something, something that startled him, and yet, that he somehow expected. For whoever the tall priest was, there could be no doubt about the short one. It was his friend from the train: the clumsy little priest with all the packages whom he had warned about his valuable possession.

Now, Valentin's mind was churning, and suddenly, the events of the day started to make sense. Valentin had learned from his visit to Scotland Yard this morning that a certain Father Brown was bringing up a silver cross filled with sapphires, a relic of some value, to show to some foreign priests at the Congress. That simpleton from the train must be Father Brown and the "valuable possession" he imprudently spoke of the silver cross.

CHAPTER SEVEN
Closing In

*N*ow there was nothing wonderful about the fact that what Valentin had found out Flambeau had also found out; Flambeau who found out everything. Also there was nothing wonderful in the fact that when Flambeau heard of a sapphire cross he should try to steal it; that was the most natural thing in all natural history. And most certainly there was nothing wonderful about the fact that Flambeau should have it all his own way with such a silly sheep as the man with the umbrella and the parcels. That bumbling priest was the sort of man whom anybody could lead on a string to the North Pole; it was not surprising that an actor like Flambeau, dressed as another priest could lead him to Hampstead Heath, a secluded and dark place for a crime.

So far, the crime seemed clear enough, and the detective felt sorry for the priest, for he seemed so helpless; and he felt angry at Flambeau for taking advantage of such a simple fellow as this priest obviously was.

Or was he? Valentin now thought about all that had happened today, and of all that had led him to his moment of triumph. He fully expected that momentarily, he would, indeed, make the arrest of the century. But as he thought about all that had happened that day, he racked his brains for the smallest rhyme or reason in it. What did stealing the blue cross have to do with throwing soup against the wall? What did it have to do with calling oranges nuts, or for paying for windows first and breaking them afterward? He had come to the end of the chase, yet somehow, he had missed the middle of it. When he failed (which was seldom) he usually had found the clue, but missed the criminal. This time, he had the criminal, but he could not grasp the clue.

The figures of the two priests could be seen in the deepening dusk, walking side-by-side, apparently in serious conversation. Perhaps they had not noticed where they were going, but they were heading for a wild and quiet part of the park. As the police followed after them, they tried to sneak up on the two, by hiding behind trees, and even crawling through deep grass. By doing so, the officers were able to get close enough to their target to hear the murmur of the priests' conversation, but no words could be distinguished except the word "reason" which they heard frequently and in a high and almost childish voice.

Once, over a little hill of land and a dense tangle of thickets, the detectives almost lost the two figures they were following. They did not find the trail again for an agonizing ten minutes, until it led to the top of a hill, overlooking a rich and desolate sunset. Under a tree in this very remote spot, was an old wooden bench. On this seat, the two priests were seated, still in serious conversation with each other. Green and gold still clung to the darkening horizon; but the dome above was turning slowly from peacock-green to peacock-blue, and the stars detached themselves more and more like solid jewels. Silently motioning to his followers, Valentin crept up right behind the big branching tree, and crouching there in total silence, he heard the words of the strange priests for the first time.

After he listened for a minute and a half, Valentin became quite doubtful. Perhaps he had dragged the two English policemen out into the night on the Heath on a false errand. For the two priests were talking about some aspect of theology just exactly like any two priests. The little short priest spoke more simply, his round face turned to the brightening stars, the other talked with his head down, as if he were not even worthy to look at them. But the innocent talk that passed between them could have been heard in any Italian cathedral or Spanish monastery.

CHAPTER EIGHT
What Was Said

*V*alentin first heard the end of one of Father
Brown's sentences, which ended, " . . . what
they really meant in the Middle Ages about the
heavens and the earth."

The taller priest nodded his bowed head and said:
"Ah, yes, these modern people appeal to their reason;
but who can look at all those stars and not feel that
there may be planets and universes above us where reason is utterly unreasonable?"

"No," said the other priest, "reason is always rea-
sonable, even in the last planet, the furthest one away. I
know that people say the Church has lowered reason,
but it is just the opposite. Alone on earth, the Church
makes reason really supreme. Alone on earth, the
Church says that God Himself is bound by reason."

The other priest raised his silent face to the starry
sky and said: "Yet who knows if in that infinite uni-
verse—?"

"Only infinite physically," said the little priest,
turning sharply in his seat, "not infinite in the sense of
escaping from the laws of truth."

Valentin, behind his tree, was biting his knuckle in
silent anger. He seemed to hear the chuckles of the
English officers he'd brought with him, laughing
because he'd brought them all this way just to listen to
the philosophical talk of these two mild old priests. In

his impatience, he didn't hear the elaborate answer of the tall priest. When he listened again, it was Father Brown who was speaking.

"Reason and justice grip even the remotest and loneliest star. Look at those stars. Don't they look as if they were single diamonds and sapphires? Even if we could see behind the very last sparkling gem out there, we would still find the words, 'Thou shalt not steal.'"

Valentin was just starting to stretch out of his cramped position, and was going to sneak away as quietly as he could, feeling that this was the most foolish chase he'd ever been on in his life. But something in the silence of the tall priest made him pause until that speaker responded. When at last he did speak, he said simply, with his head bowed and this hands on his knees: "Well, I think that other worlds may perhaps rise higher than our reason. The mystery of heaven is beyond us, and I for one, can only bow my head."

Then, with his head still bent and without changing the tone of his voice, he added: "Just hand over that sapphire cross of yours, will you? We're all alone here, and I could pull you to pieces like a rag doll."

The gentle voice and attitude added a strange

violence to that shocking change of speech. But the one who cared for the blue cross only seemed to turn his head very slightly. He still seemed to have a foolish and simple face turned to the stars. Perhaps, thought Valentin, he had not understood. Or, perhaps he had understood and was sitting utterly terrified.

"Yes," said the tall priest, in the same low voice and in the same still posture, "yes, I am Flambeau." Then, after a pause, he said: "Here, will you give me that cross?"

CHAPTER NINE
The Switch

"**N**o," said the other, and the word had an
odd sound.

Flambeau suddenly flung off all his acting.
The great robber leaned back in his seat and laughed.
"No," he cried, "you won't give it to me, you proud
priest. You won't give it to me, you little simpleton.
Shall I tell you why you won't give it to me? Because
I've got it already in my coat pocket!"

The small priest turned what seemed to be a dazed
face in the dusk, and with timid eagerness, he said:
"Are—are you sure?"

Flambeau yelled with delight. "Really, you are as
good as a comedy," he cried. "Yes, you turnip, I am
quite sure. I had the sense to switch the parcels when
you weren't looking. And now, my friend, you have
the wrong parcel, and I have the jewels. An old trick,
Father Brown—a very old trick."

"Yes," said Father Brown, and he combed his fingers through his hair with a very casual manner. "Yes,
I've heard of it before."

This chief of criminals leaned over the little country
priest with a sort of new interest. "You have heard of
it?" he asked. "Where have you heard of it?"

"Well, I mustn't tell you his name, of course," said
the little man, simply. "He came to me in confession,
you know. He had lived well and richly for about twen-

ty years entirely on the switching of brown paper packages. And so, you see, when I began to suspect you, I
thought of this poor fellow's way of doing it at once."

"Began to suspect me?" repeated the outlaw with
increased intensity. "Did you really have the nerve to
suspect me just because I brought you up to this lonely
part of the park?"

"No, no," said Father Brown with an air of apology,
"You see, I suspected you when we first met. It was
that little bulge up the sleeve where you people have
the spiked bracelet." [3]

"How in the world," cried Flambeau, "did you ever
hear of the spiked bracelet?"

"Oh, one's little flock, you know!" said Father
Brown, arching his eyebrows, "When I was pastor in
Hartlepool, there were three of my parishioners with
spiked bracelets. So, I suspected you from the first,
don't you see. I made sure that the cross should be safe,
anyhow. I'm afraid I watched you, you know. So at last
I saw you change the parcels. Then, you see, I changed
them back again. And then I left the right one behind."

"Left it behind?" repeated Flambeau, and for the
first time there was another note in his voice beside his
triumph.

"Well, it was like this," said the little priest, speaking in the same unaffected way. "I went back to that
bakery and asked if I'd left a parcel, and gave them the
address where it should be sent if it turned up. Well, I
knew I hadn't left the parcel there, but when I went
away again, I did. So, instead of running after me with
the valuable package, they have sent it in the mail to a
friend of mine in Westminster." Then he added rather

sadly, "I learned that, too, from a poor fellow in Hartlepool. He used to do it with purses he stole in the train station, but he's in a monastery now. Oh, one gets to know, you know," he added, rubbing his head again with the same sort of voice of apology. "We can't help it being priests. People come and tell us these things."

Flambeau took a brown paper parcel out of his coat pocket and tore it into pieces. There was nothing but paper and more paper inside it. He sprang to his feet with one gigantic gesture, and cried: "I don't believe you. I don't believe a bumpkin like you could manage all that. I believe you've still got the cross with you, and if you don't give it up—why we're all alone, and I'll take it by force!"

"No," said Father Brown simply, and stood up also, "you won't take it by force. First of all, because I really don't have it, and second, because we are not alone."

CHAPTER TEN
How It Was Done

Flambeau stopped in his stride forward.

"Behind that tree," said Father Brown, pointing, "are two strong policemen and the greatest detective alive. How did they come here, do you ask? Why, I brought them, of course! How did I do it? Why, I'll tell you if you like! Lord bless you, we have to know twenty such things when we work among the criminal classes in our parishes! Well, I wasn't sure you were a thief, and it would never be right to make a scandal against one of our own priests. So, I just tested you to see if anything would make you show your true self. A man generally makes a fuss if he finds salt in his coffee, if he doesn't, he has some reason for keeping quiet. I changed the sugar and salt, and you kept quiet. A man generally objects if his bill is three times too big. If he pays it, he has some reason to try not to be noticed. I altered your bill, and you paid it."

The whole world seemed to be waiting for Flambeau to leap like a tiger. But he held back as if he were under a magic spell; he was stunned with the utmost curiosity.

"Well," went on Father Brown, with great care to explain it exactly, "as you wouldn't leave any tracks for the police, of course, somebody had to. At every place we went to, I made sure that I did something that would get us noticed and talked about for the rest of the day. I didn't do much harm—a splashed wall, spilled apples, a broken window; but I saved the cross, as the cross will always be saved. It is in Westminster by now. I rather wonder why you didn't stop it with the Donkey's Whistle."

"With the what?" asked Flambeau.

"Oh, I'm glad you never heard of that," said the priest, making a face. "It's a really bad thing. I'm sure you're too good a man for a Whistler. I couldn't have fought it even with the Spots myself; I'm not strong enough in the legs."

"What on earth are you talking about?" asked the other.

"Well, I did think you'd know about the Spots," said Father Brown, agreeably surprised. "Well, you can't be so very far gone then, yet!"

"How in heaven do you know all these awful things?" cried Flambeau.

The shadow of a smile crossed the round, simple face of his priestly opponent.

"Oh, by being a priestly simpleton, I suppose," he said. "Has it never occurred to you that a man who spends his days hearing men's real sins is likely to know a bit about human evil? But, as a matter of fact, another part of my trade made me sure you weren't a priest."

"What?" asked the thief, in absolute amazement.

"You attacked reason." said Father Brown. "It's bad theology."

And even as he turned away to collect his things, the three policemen came out from under the twilight trees. Flambeau was an artist and a sportsman. He stepped back and swept Valentin a great bow.

"Do not bow to me, my friend," said Valentin, with silver clearness. "Let us both bow to our master."

And they both bowed deeply, while the little priest blinked about for his umbrella.

Footnotes

1. A Eucharistic Congress is a gathering of religious men and women. Talks are given on topics related to living the Catholic life and the importance of the Eucharist. The one that Father Brown was attending in this story is based on an actual historical event. It was the 19th Eucharistic Congress which took place in London in September, 1908.

2. Scotland Yard is the headquarters of the Metropolitan Police in London, from which national criminal investigations are coordinated.

3. The Spiked Bracelet, the Donkey's Whistle and the Spots are items that G.K. Chesterton simply made up.

Book Two

THE STRANGE FEET [1]

by G.K. Chesterton

THE STRANGE FEET

CHAPTER ONE

The Club and the Hotel

O ur story now concerns a very strange and
exclusive club for men in London called
"The Twelve True Fishermen."[2] If you were
to observe them arriving at the Vernon Hotel for their
annual club meeting, you will notice that one member, when he takes off his overcoat, is wearing a
suit which is not black, but green. You
might be wondering why his suit
is green and not black, black
being the traditional color for
gentlemen of this sort to wear.
If you had the courage and
boldness to ask this gentleman a question
(which you probably wouldn't), you
might ask him why his
suit is green. He will probably say that he does it so
that he may avoid being
mistaken for a waiter. You
will then leave, rather disappointed. But you will leave
behind you a mystery, which is as
yet unsolved, and it is a tale
worth telling.

If (to continue with this wondering game) you were to meet a mild, hard-working little priest named Father Brown, and you were to ask him what was his luckiest moment ever, he would probably say that his best luck happened at the Vernon Hotel, where he stopped a crime, and perhaps saved a soul, just by listening to a few footsteps in a hallway. He is just a little proud of this wild and wonderful guess of his, and it is possible he might tell you the story of it. But since it is unlikely that you will ever rub elbows with the members of The Twelve True Fishermen, or that you will ever walk among the criminals and the poor neighborhoods where you might find Father Brown, I am afraid you will never hear the story at all, unless you hear it from me.

The exclusive Vernon Hotel at which The Twelve True Fishermen held their annual dinners was a place that existed to serve just such a peculiar club. This hotel was so exclusive that it made its good name in a topsy-turvy way: not by attracting more customers, but actually by turning people away. There were many such fashionable restaurants and hotels in London. In one such place, no man could enter who was less than six feet tall. So groups of men would find each other, all of them over six feet, and they would eat there. There was one restaurant, where they decided to open Thursday afternoons only. So, that place was the place to be on Thursday afternoons.

Well, the Vernon Hotel was a small hotel, and it was rather difficult to find—but that was part of its charm. The restaurant's greatest inconvenience was that it, in fact, could only hold 24 people at a time. There was just one large dinner table, with a view out over a terrace, which was open to the air looking over one of the very loveliest gardens in London. So it happened that these 24 seats at this table could only be used in warm weather. This made the restaurant even more enjoyable.

The owner was a man named Mr. Lever, and he made a million out of that restaurant by making it difficult to get into. Of course, his restaurant also specialized in a quality of service that bordered on a perfect stage performance. The wines and cooking were really as good as the best in Europe. The waiters and others employed there to serve the guests were perfect for this class of Londoners. The owner knew his waiters like he knew his own children; there were 15 of them all told. It was much easier to become the president of the United States than it was to become a waiter in that hotel. Each waiter was trained in a professional silence and smoothness, as if he were the guest's servant. And, indeed, there was generally at least one waiter to every gentleman who dined.

The club of the Twelve True Fishermen could never have dined anywhere else but at the Vernon Hotel, for they wanted privacy, and would have been upset to think that other people were dining at the same restaurant as they were. On the night of their annual dinner, the Fishermen were in the habit of showing off all their treasures, especially the famous set of fish knives and forks which were, sort of, the symbol of their club. Each one was made of real silver in the shape of a fish, and in each handle was set one large, valuable pearl. These were always laid out for the fish course, and the fish course was always the best part of the meal. The Fishermen had a lot of ceremonies and special rituals, but it really had no history, and no true reason for being. You did not have to be anything in order to be a member—and unless you already were a certain sort of person, you would have never even heard of them! They had been a club for twelve years. Their president was Mr. Audley and the vice president was the Duke of Chester.

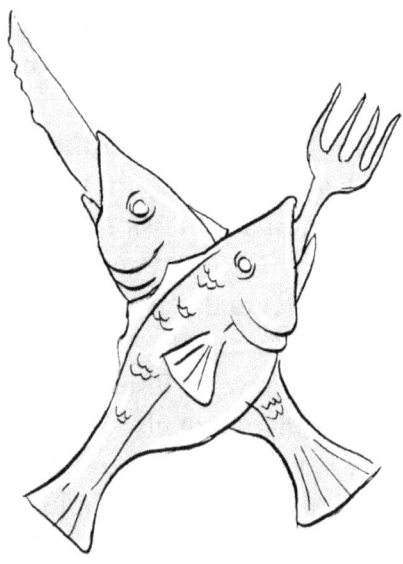

CHAPTER TWO
The Curious Sound

*N*ow, since I have told you all about this hotel and this curious club, the reader may wonder how I came to know anything about it. The reader may also wonder how an ordinary person, such as my friend Father Brown, came to find himself in that sort of place. Well, the story is really simple. One of the waiters had had a sudden heart attack, and his boss, Mr. Lever, sent for a priest because the waiter seemed to be dying. Father Brown heard his last confession, and what was said, I cannot tell you. It has nothing to do with this story and Father Brown kept that sort of information to himself. But it seems to have involved him in writing out a note or statement of some sort, to leave a message or perhaps to correct some situation.

Father Brown, therefore, asked Mr. Lever if he could sit in a quiet room somewhere, and get some paper and a pen to write down this last message. Mr. Lever had mixed feelings about this. He was a kind man, but he disliked anything out of the ordinary. He had 12 guests, who had just arrived, and he had an unusual stranger in his hotel (our Father Brown) and the priest's presence was like a spot of dirt, which Mr. Lever wanted to clean away as quickly as possible. Besides which there were no extra rooms in the tiny restaurant. People never waited in the hall, no cus-

tomers came in by chance. There were fifteen waiters.
There were twelve guests. It would be as unusual to
find a new guest at that hotel, as it would be to find
you had a new brother when you sat down to breakfast
with your own family. Not only that, but the priest's
clothes were muddy and patched; if any of Mr. Lever's
guests caught a glimpse of him, it could cause a riot.
Mr. Lever at last thought of a plan, since he had to deal
with this person without causing trouble for his dinner
guests. Down the hallway, immediately on the left, was
a corner office. Between that and the coat checkroom,
was a smaller office. In this small office sat Mr. Lever's
assistant. This small office had no direct door out.
There were two doors, however: one door led into the
larger glass office, and the other led into the coatroom.
These two connecting rooms each had exit doors.

    Into this room, Mr. Lever led Father Brown, send-
ing his assistant off on an errand.
It is a mark of his kindness that
he permitted Father Brown to sit
and write out his message. The
story Father Brown was writing
down was probably a
much better story
than this one; only
no one will ever
know it. I can
only say that
it was quite a
long message,
and that it
required the priest's

concentration, except for the last two or three paragraphs, which were not so exciting.

So, it was at the time when he had reached these last few paragraphs that the priest began to allow his thoughts to wander, and his senses, which were sharp, were suddenly awakened. It had become dark, as evening drew near, and the little room in which our priest sat had no light. As sometimes happens in the dark, the other senses become more alert, and his sense of sound was sharpened. As Father Brown was writing the last and least important part of his document, he realized that he was writing to the rhythm of a repeating noise outside, such as people sometimes sing or chant to the tune of the rail trains. When he realized what he was doing, he found out what it was: just the ordinary sound of feet walking back and forth, which in a hotel is a pretty normal thing. Still, he stared at the ceiling, listening to the sound. After he listened for a while, he rose to his feet, and listened intently, his head cocked to one side. Then he sat down again, and buried his head in his hands, now not just listening, but listening and thinking.

CHAPTER THREE
Thinking about Footsteps

*T*here was something strange about those footsteps. They were so odd that Father Brown couldn't really call them normal or abnormal. The priest followed them with his fingers on the table-top, like a man trying to learn a song on the piano.

First, there came a long rush of fast steps, such as a man might take if he were in a walking race. At a certain point they stopped and changed to a kind of slow, swinging step, long strides this time, as if the man were walking purposefully. The moment the last slow stride was done, again Father Brown would hear the rushing quick steps, and then again the heavier steps. It must have been the same pair of shoes because they had the same little squeak in them. Father Brown had the kind of brain that cannot help but ask questions; and on this particular question, his brain was hurting from the efforts of thinking. He had seen men run in order to jump. He had seen men run in order to slide. But why on earth would a man run in order to walk? Or why would he walk in order to run? Yet Father Brown could think of no other explanation for this invisible set of footsteps. The man was either walking very fast down one half of the hallway in order to walk very slowly down the other half; or he was walking very slowly at one end to have the thrill of walking fast down the other. Neither idea seemed to make much sense. Father Brown's brain was troubled.

Yet, as he began to think about it, he suddenly had a vision of these two strange feet. He let his mind wander with ideas for a few minutes. And then he suddenly knew what the slow heavy steps sounded like. They were the walk of a wealthy gentleman, and probably one who belonged to an exclusive club.

Just as he felt he was certain about his idea, the step changed to the quicker one. The priest-detective thought it sounded like a man walking quickly on tip-toe. Yet, he didn't think of it as someone doing something secretive, but it was something else—something he could not remember. He was frustrated with a half memory, the kind that is right there, but just out of reach. Surely, he had heard that strange, swift walking somewhere. Suddenly he sprang to his feet with a new idea in his head, and walked to the door. As I said before, his room had no direct door out to the hallway, but led on one side to a glass office, and on the other to the coatroom. The detective tried the door to the glass office, and found it locked. Then he looked out the window to the back of his room, and saw the beautiful purple colors of the sunset, and just for an instant, he smelled evil as a cat smells a rat.

The thinking part of him overcame those strange feelings, and he remembered that the owner had told him he would lock the door, and would come later to free him. He told himself that there were 20 things he had not thought of which might explain the strange feet outside. He reminded himself that there was enough light left and that he ought to finish the task the unfortunate waiter had left for him to do. He brought his paper to the window to catch the last of the light, and once more began to write that almost finished story. He had written for about twenty minutes, bending closer and closer to the paper to see it in the fading light; then suddenly he sat up straight. He had heard the strange feet once more.

CHAPTER FOUR

Father Brown Catches a Fish

*T*his time, they had a third strange quality. Before, the man had walked, with swiftness, yes, but he had walked. This time he ran. Father Brown could hear the swift, soft bounding steps coming along the hallway, like a panther about to pounce. Whoever was coming was a strong, active man, coming with some kind of excitement in his step. Yet, when the sound approached the glass office, it suddenly changed again into the slow, swaggering step of the gentleman.

Father Brown flung down his paper, and knowing that the office door was locked, he went to the coat-room door on the other side. The attendant on this side was temporarily absent, probably because all the guests were seated at dinner, and he was not needed at the present time. After digging his way through the over-coats, he found that the dark coatroom opened up to the well-lit hallway at a kind of half-door with a small counter on the top. The light outlined Father Brown against the sunset so that his face was darkened. But that same light shone a bright theater light upon the face of a man now standing and waiting at the counter of the coatroom door.

He was an elegant man in very plain evening clothes; quite tall, but somehow, he didn't appear to take up much room; one felt that he could have slid along with shorter men and would not have been noticed. His face, now showing in the light, was dark and lively, the face of a foreigner. He had an athletic build, his manners were perfect, but his black suit was a little shabbier than one would expect, and it bulged and bagged out in an odd sort of way. The moment he saw Father Brown's outline against the sunset, he tossed a scrap of paper with a number onto the counter and called out in an air of importance: "I want my hat and coat, please; I find I have to go away at once."

Father Brown took the paper without a word, and obediently went to look for the coat; it was not the first menial work he had done in his life. He brought it, and laid it on the counter; meanwhile the strange gentleman, who had been feeling in his pocket, said laughing: "I don't have any silver, but you can keep this," and he threw down a gold coin, and took his coat.

Father Brown remained quiet and still, but in his head was a dramatic realization; he felt like he had been struck by lightning. In that instant he suddenly was able to put two and two together and he came up with four million. It was a real inspiration. Often the Catholic Church did not approve of such revelations, and Father Brown himself did not approve of them, generally. But this was a true revelation—important in this type of rare crisis—and in this case, Father Brown acted upon it.

"I think, sir," he said politely, "that you have some silver in your pocket."

The tall gentleman stared. "Come now," he cried, "if I choose to give you gold, why should you complain?"

"Because silver is sometimes more valuable than gold," said the priest mildly; "that is, in large quantities."

The stranger looked at him curiously. Then he looked still more curiously up the hallway toward the main entrance. Then he looked back at the coatroom attendant again, and examined the window behind Father Brown's head, still colored with sunset light. Suddenly he seemed to make up his mind. He put one hand on the counter, vaulted over it as easily as an acrobat and towered over the priest, putting one huge hand upon Father Brown's collar.

"Stand still," he said in a hoarse whisper, "I don't want to threaten you, but—"

"I do want to threaten you," said Father Brown, in a voice like the rolling thunder. "I want to threaten you with the worm that dieth not, and the fire that is not quenched."

"You're a strange sort of a coat room clerk," said the other.

"I am a priest, Monsieur Flambeau,"[3] said Father Brown, "and I am ready to hear your confession."

The other stood gasping for a few moments, and then staggered into a chair.

CHAPTER FIVE
The Theft is Discovered

*T*he first two courses of the dinner of the
Twelve True Fisherman were uneventful. The
appetizers were traditionally a large spread of a
wide variety of choices. The appetizers were taken seriously, because they were useless extras, like the whole
dinner and the whole club. There was a tradition that
the soup course should be light and simple, a sort of
prelude to the fish course, which would come next.

And what was the conversation like at this meal?
Mostly, they talked of nothing at all. When they spoke
of politics, they spoke as if they were personally
acquainted with each cabinet member. They praised
some, and hated others. It seemed that politicians were
quite important to them. And yet, what was important
about them was everything except their politics. Mr.
Audley, the chairman of the Twelve True Fishermen,
was a friendly fellow, who dressed a bit old-fashioned.
He had never done anything—not even anything
wrong. He was not fast; he was not even that rich. He
was just important; that's all there was to it. The Duke
of Chester, the vice-president of the Fishermen, was a
young and rising politician. He was pleasant enough
and intelligent enough—and he was more than well off.
In public, his appearances were always successful. In
private, in a club of his own class, he was straightfor-
ward and often silly, like a school boy.

As has already been said, there were 24 seats at the terrace table and only 12 members of the club. So, they had the best seating, because all 12 could sit facing the garden, the colors of which were particularly beautiful and vivid. The chairman (Mr. Audley) sat in the middle of the table, the vice-president at the righthand end. When the 12 guests were first seated, it was the custom (for some unknown reason) for all 15 waiters to stand lining the wall like troops before a king, while the fat owner (Mr. Lever) stood and bowed to the club with a radiant smile. By the first clink of silverware, the waiters had vanished, and only one or two would appear now and then to collect plates and silverware that had been used. They were so silent they were hardly noticed.

It was time for the fish course. The Twelve True Fishermen took their famous fish knives and forks, and ate the fish in silence. When their plates were empty, the young duke made the required remark: "They can't do this anywhere but here."

"Nowhere," said Mr. Audley in a deep voice, "nowhere, except here. I was once at a café that—"

Here he was interrupted momentarily by the removal of his plate, but he was able to recover his thoughts. "I was at a café that a friend of mine claimed could do what is done here. 'Nothing like it, sir,' I told him." Audley shook his head like a judge,

" 'Nothing like it.' "

"I know that café, and that café is overrated," said Colonel Pound, speaking (by the look of him) for the first time in months.

"Oh, I don't know," said the Duke, who was an optimist, "that café is jolly good for some things. You can't beat—"

A waiter came swiftly along into the room, and then stopped dead. His stopping was as silent as his walking, but the club members were so used to the utter smoothness of the background activities of the staff, that a waiter doing anything unexpected was a jolt to their sys-

tems. They felt as you and I would feel if the world of furniture disobeyed—if a chair ran away from us.

The waiter stood staring a few seconds, while each face of the Fishermen showed a slight embarrassment. Someone could have thrown water at the waiter to wake him from his stare, but no one did. Someone could have spoken to him, but no one did. That something had gone wrong with the servants was not a thing for their concern. They wanted the thing, whatever it was, to be over. It was over. The waiter, after standing for some seconds stiffly, turned around and ran crazily out of the room.

CHAPTER SIX
Recovery

 W hen the waiter reappeared in the room, or
rather in the doorway, he had with him
another waiter, with whom he whispered and
pointed with seriousness. Then the first waiter went
away, leaving the second, and reappeared with a third
waiter. By the time a fourth waiter had joined the
group, Mr. Audley felt it was time to break the silence.
He coughed very loudly, and said: "Splendid work
young Smith is doing in India. No other nation in the
world could have—"

A fifth waiter had now walked quickly toward Mr.
Audley, and was whispering in his ear: "So sorry.
Important! Might Mr. Lever speak with you?"

The chairman turned towards the waiters, and was
amazed to see Mr. Lever approaching with quickness.
The walk of the owner was his usual walk, but his face
was by no means usual. Usually, it was a friendly warm
color; and now, it was a sickly yellow.

"You will pardon me, Mr. Audley," he said, breathlessly. "I have a great worry. Your fish plates, they are
cleared away with the knife and fork on them!"

"Well, I hope so," said the chairman, with friendli-
ness.

"You see him?" panted the excited hotel owner,
"you see the waiter who took them away? You know
him?"

"Know the waiter?" answered Mr. Audley indignantly. "Certainly not!"

Mr. Lever was in agony. "I never send him," he said. "I know not when or why he came. I send my waiter to take away the plates, and he find them already away."

Mr. Audley was bewildered, and none of the Fishermen could say anything except the quiet man—Colonel Pound—who seemed to glow with new life. He rose from his chair, leaving the rest all sitting, put his glasses on and spoke in a strange voice, as if he had just learned how to speak. "Do you mean," he said, "that somebody has stolen our set of fish silver?"

The owner was speechless, but the rest of the Fishermen were instantly on their feet.

"Are all your waiters here?" demanded the colonel, in a low harsh voice.

"Yes; they are all here. I noticed it myself," cried the young duke, pushing his boyish face into the circle. "Always count them as I come in; they look so strange up against the wall."

"But surely one cannot remember exactly, I tell you," began Mr. Audley, with hesitation.

"I remember exactly, I tell you," cried the duke excitedly. "There have never been more than 15 waiters at this place, and there were no more than 15 tonight, I'll swear; no more and no less."

The owner turned to look at the duke, shaking with surprise. "You say—you say," he stammered, "that you see all my 15 waiters?"

"As usual," agreed the duke. "What is the matter with that?"

"Nothing," said Lever, with a thickening accent, "only you did not. One of zem is dead upstairs."

There was a quiet stillness in the room for an instant. It may be (with the mention of the word "dead") that each of those men looked for a second on his own soul, and saw it as a small dried pea. One of them—the duke, I think—even said without thinking: "Is there anything we can do?"

"He has had a priest," said the owner.

Then they suddenly became aware of what had happened. The colonel flung over his chair and thumped over to the door. "If there was a fifteenth man here, friends," he said, "that fifteenth fellow is a thief. Down at once to the front and back doors and lock everything; then we'll talk. The 24 pearls of the club are worth finding."

Mr. Audley at first hesitated about whether it was gentlemanly to be in such a hurry about anything; but seeing the duke dash down the stairs with such youthful energy, he followed in a more mature fashion.

At that same instant, a sixth waiter ran into the room, and declared he had found the pile of fish plates on a side counter, with no trace of the silver.

The crowd of waiters and Fishermen then tumbled out of the dining room into the hallways and divided into two groups. Most of the Fishermen followed the owner to the front room to look at that exit. Colonel Pound, with the chairman, the vice-president, and one or two others darted down the hallway leading to the back alley—a more likely line of escape. As they did, they passed a dim room—the coatroom—and saw a short, dark-coated figure, the attendant, they thought, standing a little way back in a shadow.

"Hello, there!" called out the duke. "Have you seen anyone pass?"

The short person did not answer the question directly, but merely said: "Perhaps I have got what you are looking for, gentlemen."

They paused, wondering, while he quietly went to the back of the coatroom, and came back with both hands full of shining silver, which he laid out on the counter as calmly as a salesman. It took the form of a dozen quaintly shaped forks and knives.

CHAPTER SEVEN
The Colonel and the Priest

"You—you—" began the colonel, thrown off balance. Then he looked into the dim little room and saw two things: first, that the short dark-coated person was dressed like a priest; and second, that the window of the room behind him was broken, as if someone had jumped violently through it.

"Valuable things to leave in a coatroom, aren't they?" said the priest cheerfully.

"Did—did you steal those things?" stammered Mr. Audley, with staring eyes.

"If I did," said the little priest pleasantly, "at least I am bringing them back again."

"But you didn't," said Colonel Pound, still staring at the broken window.

"To tell the truth, I didn't," said the other, with some humor. And he seated himself rather seriously upon a stool.

"But you know who did," said the colonel.

"I don't know his real name," said the priest, evenly, "but I know a little about his weight, and a lot about his spiritual difficulties. I found out his weight when he was trying to fight me, and I found out the other when he repented."

"Oh how funny—repented!" cried the young Duke of Chester with laughter.

Father Brown got to his feet, and put his hands

behind him. "Odd, isn't it," he said, "that a thief and a wanderer should repent, when so many who are rich and content remain hard-hearted and silly, without having ever served God or man? Here, if you will excuse me, you're trespassing on my territory. If you doubt his repentance, there are your knives and forks. You are the Twelve True Fishermen, and there are all your silver fish. But He has made me a fisher of men."[4]

"Did you catch this man?" asked the colonel, frowning.

Father Brown looked at him in his frowning face. "Yes," he said, "I caught him, with an unseen hook and an invisible line which is long enough to let him wander to the ends of the earth, and still to bring him back with a little twitch upon the thread."

There was a long silence. All the other men present drifted away to carry the recovered silver back to their club members or to talk with the owner about the strange situation. But the colonel sat sideways on the counter, swinging his long legs and biting his dark moustache.

At last he said quietly to the priest: "He must have been a clever fellow, but I think I know someone else who is even more clever."

"He was a clever fellow," answered the other, "but I am not quite sure of what 'other' you mean."

"I mean you," said the colonel, with a short laugh. "I don't want to get the fellow jailed; rest easy about that. But I'd give a handful of silver forks to know exactly how you fell into this situation, and how you got the stuff out of him. I bet you're the most up-to-date fellow of all the people in this hotel here."

Father Brown seemed to like the colonel's manner—he spoke with the friendly honesty of a soldier. "Well," he said, smiling, "I can't tell you anything of the man's identity, or his own story, of course; but there's no reason why I shouldn't tell you the facts which I found out for myself."

He hopped over the counter unexpectedly and sat down next to the colonel, kicking his short legs like a little boy on a railing. He began to tell the story as easily as if he were telling it to an old friend by a Christmas fire.

"You see, Colonel," he said, "I was shut up in that small room there doing some writing, when I heard a pair of feet in this hallway doing something very strange. First came quick, funny little steps, like a man walking on tiptoe; then came slow, careless, creaking steps, as of a big man walking around with a cigar. But, the same feet made them both, I swear, and they kept coming, first fast, then slow and over again. I wondered why a man would act these two parts at once. One walk I knew; it was just like yours, Colonel. It was the walk of a gentleman waiting for something, who strolls around because he likes to keep moving. I thought I knew the other walk, too, but I could not remember what it was. What person had I seen in my travels who races along on tiptoe like that? Then, I heard the clink of plates somewhere; and the answer stood up as plain as St. Peter's. It was the walk of a waiter—the walk of a man holding plates or napkins, flying around serving his customers. Then I thought for a minute or two. And I believe I saw the kind of crime, as clearly as if I were going to commit it."

CHAPTER EIGHT

How it was Done

Colonel Pound looked at him with interest, but Father Brown's mild gray eyes were looking at the ceiling with a very empty look.

"A crime," the priest said slowly, "is like any other work of art. Don't look surprised; crimes aren't the only works of art that come from the devil's workshop. But every work of art, divine or devilish, has one unmistakable mark—I mean, that the center of it is simple, though it may end up complicated. This tale is simple, too, and it all has to do with a black coat."

The colonel looked up with some wonder.

"Yes," Father Brown said, "the whole of this tale centers on a black coat. There are other things to consider, however. First, there is a dead waiter, who was not missing in the lineup. There is the hand that cleaned up the fishplates, forks, and knives—and then disappeared. But every clever crime gets back to one simple fact, some fact that is really not very mysterious. It becomes mysterious when it is covered up, in leading men's thoughts away from it. This very large crime was built on the simple fact that a gentleman's coat is the same as a waiter's. All the rest was acting, and wonderfully good acting, too."

"Still," said the colonel, getting up and frowning at his boots, "I am not sure that I understand."

"Colonel," said Father Brown, "I am telling you that the scoundrel who stole your forks walked up and down this hallway 20 times in full light—you all saw him. He did not go and hide in dim corners where a

suspicious person might have looked for him. He kept
constantly on the move in the well-lit corridors, and
everywhere that he went, he seemed to belong there.
Don't ask me what he was like; you have seen him
yourself six or seven times tonight. You were waiting
with all the other grand people in the reception room at
the end of the passage there, with the terrace just
beyond. Whenever he came among you gentlemen, he
walked like a waiter, with quick steps, bent head, flap-
ping napkin, and flying feet. He shot out on to the
terrace, did something to the table-cloth, and shot back
again toward the office and the waiters' quarters. By the
time he had come under the eye of the office clerk and
the waiters, he had become another man in
every inch of his body, playing the part of a
gentleman. He strolled lazily among the servants with an absent-minded air, checking his
watch from time to time. It was no new
thing to them that a gentleman from the
dinner party should pace all parts of the
house like an animal at the zoo; they
know that nothing marks the wealthy
more than a habit of walking where
one chooses. The waiters assumed
he was a gentleman, you gentlemen assumed he was a waiter.
Why should you gentlemen
look at a waiter? Why should
the waiters suspect a gentleman? Once or twice he
played tricks. In the
owner's office, he called

out breezily for soda water, saying he was thirsty. He said genially that he would carry it himself, and he did; he carried it quickly and correctly among you, a waiter with an obvious errand. Of course, he could not have kept this up for very long, but he really only had to keep it up until the end of the fish course.

"His worst moment was when the waiters lined up by the wall and stood in a row. Even then he contrived to lean against the wall just round the corner in such a way that for that important instant the waiters thought him to be a gentleman, while the gentlemen thought him a waiter. The rest was easy. If any waiter caught him away from the table, that waiter saw a gentleman. He had only to go into the dining area two minutes before the fish was cleared, become a speedy servant, and clear it himself. He put the plates down on a sideboard, stuffed the silver in his breast pocket, giving it a bulgy look, and ran like a hare (I heard him coming) till he came to the coatroom. There he had only to be a gentleman—a gentleman called away suddenly on business. He had only to give his ticket to the coatroom attendant and go out again elegantly as he had come in. Only—only I happened to be the coatroom attendant."

"What did you do to him?" asked the Colonel, now totally fascinated by the story. "What did he tell you?"

"I am very sorry," said the priest, stubbornly, "but this is where the story ends."

"And an interesting story begins," muttered Colonel Pound. "I think I understand his professional trick. But I sure don't understand yours."

"I must be going," said Father Brown.

They walked together along the hallway to the front door, where they saw the fresh freckled face of the Duke of Chester, who was bounding along towards them.

"Come along, Pound," he cried breathlessly, "I've been looking for you everywhere. The dinner's on again in wonderful style, and old Audley is going to make a speech in honor of the forks being saved. We want to start a new ceremony, you know, to celebrate this occasion. Colonel Pound, my man, you got the silver back, what do you suggest?"

"Well," said the colonel, eyeing the duke with a strange look, "I would suggest that from now on, we wear green suits, instead of black. We may never know what mistakes will come up when one looks like a waiter."

"Oh, come on, Pound!" said the young man, laughing, "a gentleman never looks like a waiter!"

"And a waiter never looks like a gentleman, I suppose," said Colonel Pound, with a small grin on his face. "Father, sir, your friend must have been very clever to act so well like a gentleman."

Father Brown buttoned up his very ordinary over-coat to the neck, for the night was now stormy, and took his ordinary umbrella from a corner where it stood.

"Yes," he said, "it must be very hard work to be a gentleman; but you know, I have sometimes thought that it might be almost as hard to be a waiter."

THE STRANGE FEET

And saying "Good evening," he pushed open the heavy doors of that hotel. The doors closed behind him, and he walked quickly through the wet, dark streets in search of a bus.

Footnotes

1 This story originally appeared in a magazine called The Storyteller, in 1910, with the title "The Queer Feet."

2 London is known for its strange clubs, and Chesterton loved writing stories where he invented the strangest clubs he could think of! His craziest clubs are important in the mysteries contained in his book, The Club of Queer Trades.

3 Flambeau must have escaped prison, for he was caught in the previous story, "The Blue Cross." Chesterton gives no explanation for why Flambeau is at large.

4 This story contains a play on words. In Mark 1:17, Jesus tells Simon and Andrew he will make them fishers of men. The men in the club of "True Fishermen" in this story are only fishermen in the sense that they eat fish. Are they true fishermen, or not?

Book Three

THE FLYING STARS

by G.K. Chesterton

CHAPTER ONE

Flambeau's Last Crime

"The most beautiful crime I ever committed," Flambeau would say in his old age, "was also, by coincidence, my last. As an artist I was always trying to fit my crimes to the special season or place where I was, which is why my last crime, committed at Christmas time, was a cheery cozy, perfectly storybook Christmas crime.

"I did it in a perfectly storybook house in Putney, a house with a circular driveway, a house with a stable beside it, a house with the name on the two outer gates, a house with a monkey tree, a house with a neat and trim garden with an ornamental fence all around it. I'm sure you know the kind I'm talking about. I think my choice of crime in that setting was quite literary and ingenious. It almost seems a shame, then, that I repented that same night."

Flambeau would then proceed to tell the story from his point of view; and even from his point of view, it was odd. Viewed from the outside, it is beyond our understanding—yet it is from the outside that we must study it. From this standpoint the drama may be said to have begun when the front doors of the house opened and a young girl came out with bread to feed the birds on St. Stephen's Day.[1] She had a pretty face with brave brown eyes; but her figure was beyond imagining, for she was so wrapped up in brown furs that it was hard to say which was hair and which was fur. But for the attractive face she might have been a small toddling bear.

CHAPTER TWO

Mr. Crook

*T*he winter afternoon was reddening toward evening, and already a ruby light rolled over the bloomless beds, as it were, with ghosts of the dead roses. On one side of the house stood the stable, on the other, a narrow lane led to the larger garden behind. The young lady, having scattered bread for the birds (for the fourth or fifth time that day, because the dog ate it), walked down the lane and into a glimmering plantation of evergreens behind. Here she gave an exclamation of wonder as she looked up at the high garden wall above her where sat a young man.

"Oh, don't jump, Mr. Crook," she called out in some alarm, "it's much too high."

The person riding the wall as if in the saddle of a horse was a tall, angular young person, with dark hair sticking up like a brush—he was intelligent looking, but pale. His pale face seemed all the more so because he had on a bright red tie, the only

part of his clothing which he seemed to have made an effort about. Perhaps the tie meant something. He took no notice of the girl's alarm, but leapt like a grasshopper to the ground next to her, where he very well could have broken his leg.

"I think I should have been a burglar," he said simply, "and I probably would be one if I hadn't been born in that nice house next door. I can't see any harm in being a burglar."

"How can you talk like that?" the young lady scolded him.

"Well," said the young man, "if you're born on the wrong side of the wall, I can't see that it's wrong to climb over it."

"I never know what you will say or do next," she said.

"I often don't know myself," replied Mr. Crook; "but then, I am on the right side of the wall now."

"And which is the right side of the wall?" asked the young lady, smiling.

"Whichever side you are on," said the young man named Crook. She blushed and took his arm.

As they walked together down the path and toward the front garden, they heard a car's horn honk three times, each time coming nearer and nearer. Soon the elegant pale green car came into view in front of the house.

"Hello, hello!" said the young man with the red tie, "here's a man born on the right side of the wall. I didn't know, Miss Adams, that your Santa came in a car these days. So modern!"

"Oh, that's my godfather, Sir Leopold Fischer. He

always comes on St. Stephen's day."

Then, after an innocent pause, which betrayed some lack of enthusiasm, Ruby Adams added:

"He is very kind."

John Crook, journalist, had heard of that famous government official, Fischer; and it was not his fault the famous government official had not heard of John Crook. But he said nothing and grimly watched the unloading of the car, which was a rather long process. A large, neat chauffeur in green got out from the front, and a small, neat manservant in gray got out from the back, and between them they deposited Sir Leopold on the doorstep and began to unpack him like some very carefully protected parcel. Rugs enough to stock a bazaar, furs of all the beasts of the forest, and scarves of all the colors of the rainbow were unwrapped one by one till they revealed something resembling the human form; the form of a friendly, but foreign-looking old gentleman with a gray goat-like beard and a beaming smile.

CHAPTER THREE

Sir Leopold and the Flying Stars

*N*ow the inner doors of the home were opened and Colonel Adams (father of the young lady) came out to invite his important guest inside. Adams was a tall, sun burnt, and very silent man who wore a strange red smoking cap that made him look like an Egyptian Pasha.[2] With him was his brother-in-law from Canada, a big and rather boisterous young gentleman farmer with a yellow beard named James Blount. With him also, was a very ordinary-looking person, a priest from the neighborhood Catholic Church; for the colonel's wife, who had died, had been Catholic, and the children, as usually happens in such cases, had been raised Catholic. Everything about the priest seemed common, right down to his name, which was Brown; yet the colonel always enjoyed his company, and frequently asked him to such family gatherings.

And now everyone was being introduced to Sir Leopold, from the ordinary Father Brown to the gloomy Mr. Crook. The famous man, however, soon began struggling with his coat as if searching for something. At length he drew out of his inner pocket a black oval case which he explained was his Christmas present for his goddaughter. As he held out the case before them all, it flew open at a touch and half-blinded them. It was just as if a crystal fountain had spurted in their eyes. In a nest of orange velvet lay three white and sparkling diamonds that seemed to set the very air on fire all round them. Sir Leopold smiled kindly, enjoying the surprise and the delight of the girl, the admiration and gruff thanks of the colonel, and the astonishment of the whole group.

"I'll put them back away, now, my dear," said Sir Leopold, closing the case and putting them back in his pocket. "I had to be careful of them as I traveled here. They're the three great African diamonds called 'The Flying Stars,' because they've been stolen so often. All the big criminals are after these; but even the worst men on the streets and back alleys want to get their hands on them. I might have had them stolen right on the road here. It was quite possible."

"Quite natural," growled the young man with the red tie, "I wouldn't blame them if they had taken them. When they ask for bread, and you don't give them a stone, I think they might take the stone for themselves." (Here our young friend was referring to a Bible verse you may be familiar with, although using it in a rather upside-down way, as you can see.)

"I won't let you talk like that," cried Ruby, who was glowing with the idea of the diamonds. "You're only saying that because you call yourself a horrible—whatever-you-call-it. You know what I mean. What do you call a man who wants to hug a chimney sweep?"

"A saint," said Father Brown.

"I think," said Sir Leopold, with a ridiculous smile, "that Ruby means a Socialist."[3]

"I have absolutely no desire to hug a chimney sweep," said Mr. Crook with impatience. "A Socialist is someone who wants all the chimneys swept, and all the chimney sweeps paid for doing the job."

"But who won't allow you," said the priest in a low voice, "to own your own soot." (Father Brown was referring to the Socialist's belief that no one should own land.)

Crook looked at the priest with an eye of interest and even respect. "Does a person want to own his own soot?" he asked.

"He might," answered Father Brown, with a gleam in his eye. "I've heard that gardeners use it in their compost. And I once made six children happy at Christmas time when the magician didn't show up, just with soot—applied to my face, that is."

"Oh, splendid," cried Ruby, "Oh, I wish you would do it now, for us."

The noisy Canadian, Mr. Blount, was loudly applauding and the amazed Sir Leopold was also voicing his approval when there was a knock at the front door.

CHAPTER FOUR
A Play is Proposed

*T*he front doors were opened again and they showed the front garden of evergreens, monkey tree and all, now gathering gloom against a gorgeous violet sunset. The scene, framed in the doorway was so colorful and stunning, like a backdrop to a play, that they almost didn't see the figure standing in the doorway. He was dusty-looking and in a frayed coat, evidently a common messenger. "Are any of you Mr. Blount?" he asked and held out a letter doubtfully. Mr. Blount stopped amid his urging of Father Brown and opened the envelope. With evident astonishment he read the letter. His face clouded a little, and then cleared. He turned to his brother-in-law, the host, Colonel Adams.

"Colonel, I'm already a guest in your house, and I don't want to be a nuisance," he said with a cheery voice; "but would it upset you if an old friend of mine dropped in to visit me here tonight on business? As a matter of fact, he's Florian, the famous French acrobat and actor; I knew him years ago in Canada, as he was born a French Canadian, and he seems to have business with me, though I can't guess what it is."

"Of course, of course," replied the colonel. "My dear friend, any friend of yours is welcome here. Perhaps he will help us celebrate this, ah, celebration."

"He'll put the soot on his face, if that's what you

mean," cried Blount, laughing. "He's the actor for that."

"Well, well," said Crook, "what will happen now?"

"Let's have a wonderful evening, I say," said Blount. "Why don't we play a game of charades tonight, or put on a pantomime?"[4]

Blount continued, "I saw a pantomime once when I was twelve years old, and I've always remembered it, though it seems that they don't perform them anymore around here. Everything now is just serious plays and silly love stuff. Let's do the one where the ballerina falls in love with the harlequin,[5] and her father is against it, and the father's servant tries to break it up, and the policeman gets caught in the middle of it all. How about it?"

CHAPTER FIVE
A Play is Planned

"*H*ow shall we do it?" asked Crook, moodily. Mr. Crook was not quite in favor of acting.

"It's simple," said Blount, "we can use things found around the house, a table, a laundry basket, plates and cups, things like that."

"That's true," said Crook, warming to the idea as he began to think. He nodded eagerly, and began to walk around as he spoke. "But I must have a policeman's uniform for my part, and I'm afraid I haven't been able to break into the police headquarters lately, or else I'd have a stolen uniform in my closet. How will I get my costume?"

Blount frowned thoughtfully for a moment, and then slapped his thigh. "I've got it!" he cried. "I have Florian's address here, and he knows every costume shop in London. I'll call him and tell him to bring a policeman's costume when he comes." And he went quickly off to make the call.

"Oh, it's wonderful, godfather," cried Ruby, almost dancing. "I'll be the ballerina who falls in love with the harlequin, and you can be Poppins, the angry father who doesn't want me to marry him."

The millionaire looked at his goddaughter as if she had asked him to proclaim a false creed. "I think, my dear," he said, "you will have to get someone else to play Poppins."

"I will be Poppins if you like," said Colonel Adams, taking his cigar out of his mouth, and speaking for the first and last time.

The Canadian came into the room cheerfully, as he reported on his phone call. "There, we're all set. Mr. Crook will be the clown; he's a journalist, and he knows all the old jokes. I can be the harlequin, you only need long legs and to jump around a lot. My friend Florian says he's bringing the police costume; he's changing along the way. Ruby can be the ballerina who'll be beautiful, and everyone else can be the audience. We'll pretend that the clown is Poppins' servant, who gets the policeman to prevent a fight between the harlequin and the ballerina's father. Won't that be funny? We can act it all out in the hall; the audience can sit on those steps there, one row above another. These front doors can be the background scenery, either open or shut. Shut, it will be the inside of an English home. Open, a moonlit garden. It all goes by magic." And snatching a piece of chalk out of his pocket, he made a line across the hall floor, halfway between the front door and the staircase, to mark the end of the stage.

How they got such a banquet of silliness ready for the ridiculous little play remained a mystery. But they went at it with that mixture of reckless excitement and energy that lives when young people are in a house; and youth was in that house that night, though not all may have guessed from which two hearts this happy atmosphere flowed. As usually happens on such occasions, things got wilder and wilder. The ballerina looked lovely in a skirt that strangely resembled the large lampshade in the drawing room. The clown and

Poppins made themselves white with flour from the cook, and red with rouge from another female servant, who remained (like all true Christian donors) anonymous. The harlequin, already clad in silver—which looked like aluminum foil taken from the kitchen—was trying to get the crystals out of the chandelier so that he could really shine. In fact he would have done so, but Ruby gave him instead some old costume jewelry she had once worn when she dressed as the Queen of Diamonds at a fancy-dress party.

Indeed her uncle, James Blount, was getting almost out of hand in his excitement. He was like a schoolboy. He put a paper donkey's head unexpectedly on Father Brown, who bore it patiently and even found a way to make the ears move. Blount then put the paper donkey's tail on the jacket of Sir Leopold. Ruby, however, frowned on this. "Uncle is too silly," she cried to Crook, round whose shoulders she had seriously placed a string of sausages. "Why is he so wild?"

"How should I know? He is the harlequin in love with you, the ballerina," said Crook. "I am only the clown who makes old jokes."

CHAPTER SIX
A Play is Performed

"*I* wish you were the harlequin," she said, giving her friend, Mr. Crook, a quick little kiss on the cheek, leaving him with his clown's hat slightly tipped over one ear.

Father Brown, though he knew all the details of all the preparations that took place behind the scenes, became part of the audience. He went around to the stairs, and sat among the audience with a serious expression of expectation on his face, like a child who is just attending his first play. The audience was small, relatives, mostly, a few neighbors who came over at the last minute, and the servants. Sir Leopold sat in the front row seat, his full and large figure partly obscuring the view for the little priest behind him. The show started in utter confusion, yet it brought some laughs and was not too terrible. There was a lot of improvisation, mostly coming from Crook the clown. He was usually a clever man, but tonight he was inspired to bring laughs with quicker than usual wit, cracking jokes right and left, as he looked for the approval of a certain ballerina who waited stage right. Perhaps it was she who was his inspiration. He was supposed to be the clown, but he was really almost everything else, the author (as much as there was an author), the prompter, the scene painter, the scene changer, and also the orchestra. At sudden moments in the outrageous performance, he would suddenly throw himself in full costume at the piano, where he would bang out some popular music equally silly and appropriate for this silly performance.

The height of all this was the moment when the two front doors at the back of the scene flew open, showing the lovely moonlit garden, but also showing their eagerly awaited and professional guest: the great Florian, dressed as a policeman. The clown at the piano played a spy theme from some movie, but it was drowned out by the applause, for everything the great actor did was exactly like what a real policeman would have done. The harlequin leaped at the policeman and tried to fight with him, for the policeman was supposed to take the side of the clown and Poppins, and arrest the harlequin. He fought, he joked, the piano player played funny songs, the policeman looked at the audience with a well-acted look of astonishment, and then the harlequin gave a great leap, flying right into the arms of the surprised policeman, who fell to the floor amid the laughter and applause of the audience—and the piano player played a silly tune to go along with it all. Then, the famous actor gave an amazing impression of a man who has fainted, and lay quite still for a long time. It was almost impossible to believe that a living person could appear so limp.

CHAPTER SEVEN
The Theft

*T*he athletic harlequin swung the policeman around like a sack of potatoes, while the clown pounded out crazy tunes on the piano. When the harlequin lifted the policeman off the floor, the clown played, "I arise from dreams of thee." When the harlequin finally let fall the policeman with a convincing thud, the clown played this jingle: "I sent a letter to my love and on the way I dropped it." Just then, Father Brown's view was blocked—he could no longer see the stage because Sir Leopold, who was sitting in front of him, stood up and thrust his hands savagely into all his pockets. Then he sat down nervously, still fumbling, and then stood up again. For an instant it seemed seriously likely that he would run onto the stage. He turned to stare at the clown playing the piano and then burst in silence out of the room.

The priest watched for a few more minutes the dance of the harlequin who was celebrating the defeat of the policeman. With real art, the harlequin danced slowly backward out of the door into the garden, which was full of moonlight and stillness. His costume of silver paper and paste jewels, which had been too glaring onstage, looked more magical and silvery as it danced away under a brilliant moon. The audience was about to break into applause when Father Brown felt someone touch his arm, and he was asked in a whisper to come to the colonel's study.

He followed his messenger with a feeling of increasing suspicion, which was not dispelled as he gazed upon the almost comical scene in the study. There sat Colonel Adams, still in his ridiculous costume as Poppins, but with the saddest of eyes. Sir Leopold Fisher was leaning against the mantle and heaving with all the importance of panic.

"This is a very painful matter, Father Brown," said Adams. "It seems those diamonds, which we all saw this afternoon, appear to have vanished from my friend's coat pocket. And as you—"

"As I," interrupted Father Brown with a smile, "was sitting just behind him—"

"No, we're not suggesting that," said Adams, with a nod to Sir Leopold, which implied that something maybe *had* been suggested. "I only ask you to give me some help here."

"If you mean shall I show you what is in my pockets? Gladly," said Father Brown, and proceeded to do this, displaying a few quarters and pennies, a bus ticket, a small silver crucifix, a small prayer book, and a stick of gum.

The colonel looked at him for a long moment, and then said, "You know, I would like to see the inside of your head more than the inside of your pockets. My daughter is one of your people, a Catholic, I know; well, she has lately—"

"She has," cried out Sir Leopold, "let into the house a Socialist who said to us all that he would steal anything from a rich man. So, here we are, and here is a rich man," he said, pointing to himself.

"If you want the inside of my head, you can have it," said Father Brown, rather wearily "for what it's worth, and you can tell me after I speak if it's worth anything at all. But the first thing my mind thinks of, is that men who steal diamonds don't talk about Socialism. They are, in reality, more likely to criticize it."

The others moved uncomfortably in their chairs, and the priest went on.

"You know, Socialists are people we see every day, they are regular people, more or less. A Socialist would never steal a diamond, any more than he might steal a church. We should look for a man we don't know. The man who was acting the policeman—Florian, where is he this minute, I wonder?"

CHAPTER EIGHT
The Policeman

*P*oppins sprang up to his feet instantly and walked rapidly out of the room. A short time of quiet passed, during which the millionaire stared at the priest and the priest stared at his prayer book; then Poppins returned and said with all seriousness, "The policeman is still lying on the stage. The curtain has gone up and down five or six times; he is still lying there."

Father Brown dropped his book and stood staring with a look of worry. Very slowly, he seemed to come to life, and then he said the thing they least expected.

"Please forgive me, colonel, but when did your wife die?"

"My wife!" replied the soldier, "she died two months ago, for heaven's sake, why? And her brother James Blount arrived one week too late to see her, unfortunately."

The priest shot up like a cannon. "Come on!" he shouted with quite a lot of excitement. "Come on! We've got to go and look at that policeman!"

They hurried out to the stage, rushing impolitely past the ballerina and the clown (who were whispering to each other quite happily), and Father Brown bent over the policeman lying there.

"Chloroform, I smell it. He's been drugged," he said as he rose. "I only just guessed it a moment ago."

There was a silent stillness, and then the colonel said slowly, "Please, please tell us what this all means."

Father Brown suddenly laughed out loud, then stopped, and struggled to compose himself so he could speak. "Gentlemen," he gasped, "there's not much time for talk. I must run after the criminal. But this great French actor who played the policeman—this very clever sleeping policeman that the harlequin was teasing and joking with—he was—" his voice again failed him, and he turned and started to run.

"He was . . .?" Sir Leopold called after him.

"A real policeman!" cried Father Brown as he ran away into the night.

There were trees and shrubs at the end of that leafy garden, in which the laurels showed against a sapphire sky and silver moon, even in that midwinter, warm colors as of the south. The green gaiety of the waving laurels, the rich purple of the night, the moon like a huge crystal, make a breathtaking picture; and among the top branches of the garden trees a strange figure is climbing—he doesn't look beautiful, really; incredible is more like it. He sparkles from head to toe as if clad in 10 million brilliant shining moons; the real moon catches him at every movement and sets a new inch of him on fire. But he swings, flashing and successful, from the short tree in this garden to the tall tree in the other, and only stops because a shadow has appeared under the smaller tree and has called to him.

CHAPTER NINE
Silver Bird in a Green Cage

"Well, Flambeau," says the voice, "you really look like a Flying Star; but you'll be a Falling Star soon."

The silver, sparkling harlequin leaned forward in the leaves and branches, confident of his escape, and listened to the little priest below.

"You never did anything better, Flambeau. It was very clever to come here from Canada just a week after Mrs. Adams died, when no one was in the mood to wonder if she really had a brother. It was even cleverer of you to have known about the Flying Stars and the day of Sir Leopold's coming. But, there's no cleverness, instead pure genius, in the rest of it. Stealing diamonds, I suppose, was nothing to you. You could have done it in a hundred ways, other than pretending to pin a donkey's tail on Sir Leopold so that you had the chance to reach into his pocket. But, the whole rest of it, I must admit, was your very best work."

The silvery figure among the green leaves lingered as if mesmerized by the voice, though his escape was easily there right behind him; yet he was staring at the man below him.

"Oh, yes," said the priest below, "I know all about it. I know you not only made everyone perform in the pantomime, but you put it to double use. You were going to steal the diamonds quietly. Then news came from a friend of yours that you were suspected here, and that a policeman was already on his way to arrest you this very night. A common thief would have heeded the warning, and run away as fast as he could. But you are a thief *and* a poet. You had the clever idea of hiding the jewels in the midst of all of your fake stage gems. You saw that if you were the harlequin, the policeman would fit right into the play. When the officer from the Putney police station set off to find you, he walked into the strangest trap ever set in this world. When the front door opened, he walked right on to the stage of a Christmas pantomime, where he would be the object of jokes and physical comedy, amid the roar of laughter and applause of the most respectable people in Putney. Oh, you could never do anything better. And now, by the way, you might as well give me back those diamonds."

The green branch on which the harlequin sat bounced up and down a little bit, as he balanced up there; but the voice went on:

"I want you to give them back, Flambeau, and I want you to give up this life. You are still young, and there is honor and humor in you, but they won't last if you continue in this thieving lifestyle. A good man may stay at a certain level of goodness. But an evil man can never stay at one level of evil. The road always goes down and down. Many a man I've known started out like you, to be an honest outlaw, a Robin Hood; a merry robber of the rich—and ended up stuck in the mud and dirt of the life of crime. I know the woods behind you look very free, Flambeau; I know that in a flash you could melt into them as easily as a monkey.

But some day you will be an old gray monkey, Flambeau. You'll wake up alone in a free forest, cold at heart and close to death, and everything around you bare and still."

CHAPTER TEN

The Stars Fly

Everything continued to be still, as if the small man below held the man in the trees by an invisible string, a string made of the thief's curiosity about the thoughts of the priest. The priest went on:

"You've begun a downward slide already. You used to boast that you never did a crime that hurt anyone. But tonight, you've hurt someone. You've left all the suspicion for this crime on a young man who is honest and kind, and you are separating him from the young lady whom he loves, and who loves him. If you continue on like this, your deeds will hurt others more and more."

Slowly, as in a moonlit dream, the three diamonds fell one after another from the tree down to the grass. The priest bent over to pick them up, and when he looked up again the green cage of the tree was emptied of its silver bird.

The restoration of the gems (accidentally picked up by Father Brown, of all people) let the evening end in triumph. Sir Leopold, who now was in a very good mood, even told the priest that though he (Sir Leopold, that is) was an intelligent and scientific thinker who was beyond what religion had to offer, he could respect someone whose beliefs required him to be shut off from "real life" and ignorant of the ways of the world.

Footnotes

1 St. Stephen's Day – this is the day after Christmas. In England it is called Boxing Day. There are many traditional activities in England on this day.

2 Pasha – honorary title formerly given to officers of high rank in Turkey or Egypt

3 Socialist – a person who believes in a particular political system where the government or the community owns property and businesses. In this system there is no personal wealth or property.

4 Pantomime – a play in which the actors do not speak. It can be accompanied by music.

5 Harlequin – a comic character in a play; like a clown, usually masked and wearing a multi-colored diamond patterned.

Book Four

THE ABSENCE
OF MR. GLASS

by G. K. Chesterton

CHAPTER ONE

Dr. Hood

D r. Orion Hood, the famous and well-respected criminologist,[1] stood looking at the sea out one of the large picture windows of his office. The sea was beautiful today, swelling like an endless wall of blue green marble. Dr. Hood never tired of gazing upon the view of the sea. He turned to his office, luxurious and tidy, with everything in its place. He prided himself on having the finest and most expensive cigars and the finest and most excellent brands of whiskey, but next to these stood bookshelves with the great classics of English literature and poetry. He was a man of refined and expensive tastes.

There were also various instruments such as a scientist of this type would have: a microscope, some chemistry equipment, and other such things as would be needed to solve a crime.

Dr. Orion Hood began to pace back and forth restlessly, as if considering a serious situation. He was dressed neatly, his hair well combed and streaked with quite a bit of grey, though it was thick and healthy. His face was lean, but serious and expectant. Everything about him and his room indicated something at once rigid and restless, like the great northern sea next to which he had built his office.

There was a knock at the door, a call to come in, and now, there was in the office of Dr. Hood the very opposite of all that we have thus far described. A small shapeless little figure, who seemed to find his own hat and umbrella as difficult to manage as a large piece of luggage, shuffled into the room. The umbrella was a black bundle long past repair; the hat was a broad-curved black hat common to priests, but uncommon in England. The man was the embodiment of all that is homely and helpless.

CHAPTER TWO
Father Brown meets Dr. Hood

*T*he doctor observed the newcomer with restrained astonishment, as if some huge but obviously harmless sea creature had crawled into the room. The newcomer watched the doctor with a smile that showed his gratitude in having found what he was looking for. However, as he tipped his head in greeting, his hat fell to the carpet and his umbrella slipped to his feet with a thud. He reached for the one and ducked after the other, but with the smile still on his round face he spoke at the same time the following:

"My name is Brown. Please excuse me. I have come to see you about the MacNabs. I've heard you often help people out of such troubles. Please excuse me if I am wrong."

By this time, he had recovered the hat and picked up the umbrella, and was now bowing before the doctor to correct the greeting at last.

"I don't know what you are talking about," replied the scientist with seriousness. "I am afraid you have come to the wrong office door. I am Dr. Hood, and my work relates to teaching and writing. It is true that occasionally I am consulted by the police on difficult or unusual matters, but—"

"Oh, this is quite difficult, and unusual," interrupted the little man called Brown. "After all, her mother won't let them get engaged." He sat back in the chair he had taken and his face had a bright glow.

The eyebrows of Dr. Hood drew together darkly, but the eyes under them were bright with something that could either be anger or amusement. "Still," he said, "I don't understand."

"You see, they want to get married," said the man with the clerical hat. "Maggie MacNab and young Todhunter want to get *married*. Now, what can be more important than that?"

The great Orion Hood's scientific accomplishments had deprived him of many things—some said it was his health, others said it was God; but he still had a good sense of humor. At the last words of the innocent little priest, a laugh escaped from deep inside the doctor, and he threw himself into an armchair with the air of a consulting physician.

"Mr. Brown," he said gravely, "it has been fourteen and a half years since I was asked about a personal problem; then it was a case of an attempt to poison the French president. Now, as I understand it, you have some friend named Maggie, and you wonder if a man named Todhunter is the person she should marry. And somewhere in there, the person named Maggie has a mother who does not wish these two to marry. Well now, Mr. Brown, I am a sportsman. I will take this on. I will give the MacNab family my best advice, as good as I gave the country of France and King of England— no, better, fourteen years better. I have nothing else to do this afternoon. Tell me your story."

CHAPTER THREE
The Story

So it was that the little clergyman called Brown thanked the doctor with warmth and unusual simplicity. And, with hardly a pause after his thanks, he began his story: "I told you my name is Brown; well that's a fact, and I'm the priest of the little Catholic Church I dare say you've seen beyond those straggly streets, where the town ends toward the north. In the last and straggliest of those streets which run along the sea, there is a very honest but rather sharp-tempered member of my flock, a widow called MacNab. She has one daughter, and she runs a boarding house, and between her and the daughter, and between her and the renters—well I dare say there is a great deal to be said on both sides. At present she has only one renter, the young man called Todhunter; but he has given more trouble than all the rest, for he wants to marry the young woman of the house."

"And the young woman of the house," asked Dr. Hood, with a huge and silent amusement, "what does she want?"

"Well, she wants to marry him," cried Father Brown, sitting up eagerly. "That is just the awful complication."

"This is indeed a difficult puzzle," said Dr. Hood.

"The young James Todhunter," continued the priest, "is a very decent man so far as I know; but then nobody knows very much. He is a bright, fair person, agile like a monkey, clean-shaven like an actor, and as polite as a messenger boy. He seems to have money, but nobody knows what his line of work is. Mrs. MacNab, therefore (being a pessimistic kind of person), is sure that his work must be something awful, like explosives. The explosives must be the shy and silent type, though, for the fellow just shuts his door for several hours of the day and studies something behind the locked door. He tells them his seclusion is only temporary and that it is for a certain purpose, and he promises to explain it all before the wedding. That is all that anyone knows for certain, but Mrs. MacNab will tell you a lot more. You know how stories grow. There is a story of two voices talking in the room, though when the door is opened, Todhunter is always alone. There are stories of a mysterious tall man in a top hat, who once came out of the mists of the sea, stepping softly across the sandy fields and through the small back garden at twilight, until he was heard talking to the hotel guest at his open back window.

"The conversation seemed to end in a quarrel. Todhunter closed his window down with a bang, and the man in the high hat had melted back into the fog again. This story is told by the family with the deepest sense of mystery, but I really suspect that Mrs. MacNab thinks that the Other Man (or whatever it is) crawls out every night from a big box which Todhunter keeps in the corner of his room, locked up all day. You can see, Dr. Hood, how this locked door of Todhunter's is food for the imagination. And yet, this young man looks respectable, and he is always on time, and looks so innocent. He always pays his rent, right on time; he rarely drinks; he is always kind to the younger children, and can keep them amused all day; and last and most important of all, he is as popular with the older daughter as he is with the children, and the daughter is ready to go to church with him tomorrow."

A man who is used to using his intellect on large problems is pleased and proud to use his brain on a little problem. The great specialist, having brought himself down to the simple level of the country priest, put his whole heart into the simpleton's problem. He settled himself into his armchair and began to talk in the tone he might have used to give a familiar lecture:

"Even in the smallest situation, it is best to look first at the natural tendencies of things. A certain flower may not be dead yet in early winter, but all the flowers are dying; a certain pebble may not be wet with the tide, but the tide is now coming in. To the scientific eye, human history is a series of comings and goings, like the tides, or the birds flying south and returning north. Some people, like these MacNabs, for instance, may believe in superstition. The scared Mrs. MacNab hears voices from the sea, but the scientific man sees the history of such people, and their superstitions, and he sees—"

Before the scientist could finish his sentence, there was a sound from the hallway, and the swishing of a lady's skirt, and the door opened to a young girl, dressed well, but disordered in her appearance and red-hot with haste. She had sea-blown blond hair, and was beautiful with red cheeks over her high cheekbones. She apologized abruptly.

"I'm sorry to interrupt you, sir," she said, "but I had to follow Father Brown here; it's a matter of life and death."

CHAPTER FOUR

The Death of Mr. Todhunter

ather Brown sprang to his feet, sending his umbrella and hat flying. "What's happening, Maggie?" he said.

"James has been killed, as far as I can tell," answered the girl, still breathing hard from her rush. "That man Glass has been with him again; I heard them talking through the door quite plainly. Two separate voices; for James speaks low, and the other voice was high and quavery."

"That man 'Glass'?" repeated the priest in some confusion.

"I know his name is Glass," answered the girl, with great impatience. "I heard it through the door. They were quarrelling—about money, I think—for I heard James say again and again, 'That's right, Mr. Glass,' or 'No, Mr. Glass,' and then 'Two and three, Mr. Glass.' But we're talking too much; you must come at once, while there may be time left."

"Time for what?" asked Dr. Hood, who had been studying the young lady with interest. "What is there about Mr. Glass and his money troubles that should cause such urgency?"

"I tried to break down the door and couldn't," answered the girl impatiently. "Then I ran around to the back yard, and managed to climb on to the window sill and I looked into the room. It was dark, and seemed to be empty, but I swear I saw James lying huddled up in a corner, as if he were tied up."

"This is very serious," said Father Brown, gathering up his wayward hat and umbrella and standing up. "As a matter of fact, I was just discussing your situation with this gentleman, and his view—"

"Has been changed dramatically," said the scientist seriously. "I don't think this lady is as superstitious as I suspected. And, because I have nothing else to do, I will put on my hat and go into town with you."

In a few minutes all three were approaching the dreary street where the MacNabs lived: the girl with the stern and breathless stride of a mountain climber; the criminologist with a lounging grace (which was not without a certain leopard-like swiftness); and the priest at an energetic trot entirely without distinction. The aspect of this edge of the town was desolate. The scattered houses stood farther and farther apart in a broken string along the seashore; the afternoon was closing with a premature and somewhat murky twilight. The sea was an inky purple and murmuring ominously. In the scrappy back garden of the MacNabs which ran down toward the sand, two black, barren-looking trees stood up like demon hands held up in astonishment. As Mrs. MacNab ran down the street to meet them, with lean hands spread like the trees and her fierce face in shadow, she was like a demon herself.

The doctor and the priest made scant reply to her shrill account of her daughter's story, with more disturbing details of her own. They endured her vows of vengeance against Mr. Glass for murdering, and against Mr. Todhunter for being murdered, or against the latter for having dared to want to marry her daughter, and then not having lived to do it. They passed through the narrow passage in the front of the house until they came to the lodger's door at the back, and there Dr. Hood, with the trick of an old detective, put his shoulder sharply to the panel and burst in the door.

The door opened on a scene of catastrophe. No one seeing that room, even for just a moment, could doubt that in that room, there must have been a fight between two, or perhaps more, persons. A deck of cards was littered across the table and all over the floor as if a game had been interrupted. Two wine glasses stood ready for wine on a side table, but a third glass lay smashed in a star-shaped pattern of crystal on the carpet. A few feet from that was what looked like a long knife, or a short sword, straight, but with a fancy decorated handle. In one corner of the room, a man's silk hat had rolled, just as if it had been knocked off someone's head. And in the other corner, thrown like a sack of potatoes, but tied up like a bundle of mail, lay Mr. James Todhunter, with a scarf tied across his mouth, and six or seven ropes tied in knots around his elbows and ankles. His brown eyes were alive and looked around alertly.

CHAPTER FIVE
The Crime Scene

*D*r. Orion Hood paused for a second on the doormat and took in the whole violent scene. Then he stepped quickly across the carpet and picked up the man's silk hat, and seriously put it on the head of the still tied Todhunter. It was much too large for him, so that it slipped down on to his shoulders.

"Mr. Glass's hat," said the doctor, taking it up and looking at it with a magnifying glass he had taken from his pocket. "How can we explain the absence of Mr. Glass, and the presence of Mr. Glass's hat? For Mr. Glass is obviously very careful with his clothes. This hat is of a make and style which is very elegant, though not very new. An old gentleman, I suppose."

"But good heavens!" called out Miss MacNab, "aren't you going to untie the man first?"

"I say 'old' with a partial degree of certainty," continued the scientist, "and my reason may seem a little far-fetched. The hair on the head of a human falls out in different degrees for different men, but it always falls

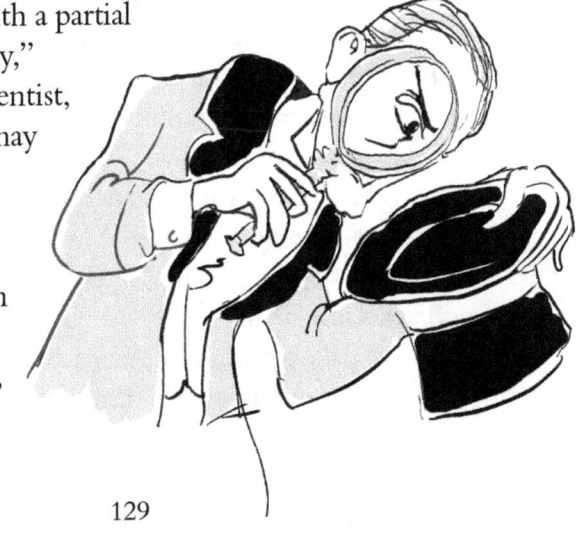

out. And with my magnifying glass, I *should* have seen tiny hairs in a hat which had recently been worn. I saw none on this hat, which leads me to guess that Mr. Glass is bald. Now, when I consider this along with the high and quavering voice which Miss MacNab heard and described so vividly—patience, my dear lady, patience—I conclude that Mr. Glass is an older, mature man. I would also guess that he is rather strong, even though old, and he must be rather tall. This I guess from the evidence the lady gave of a 'tall man in a silk hat at the window' but I think I can guess it even for myself. This wine glass has been smashed all over the place, but one of the pieces is lying here, on the mantle. A fragment of the glass could never have fallen there if the wine glass had been smashed by someone as short as Mr. Todhunter."

"By the way," said Father Brown, "couldn't we untie Mr. Todhunter?"

"Our lesson from the wine glasses doesn't end here," continued the scientific specialist. "I could also add that the man Mr. Glass is bald or nervous as a result of bad habits rather than age. Mr. Todhunter, as some-one said earlier, is a quiet gentleman, one who rarely drinks. These cards and wine glasses can't be a normal part of his room decorations; they must have been put out for the visitor. I can go even farther in my thoughts. Mr. Todhunter may or may not have had these glasses, but can we even see any wine? What were these glasses to contain then? I would suggest brandy or whiskey, or perhaps some drink which Mr. Glass brought with him. Now we have a picture of the man, or at least of his type of person: tall, elderly, fashionable, someone who likes to play card games and drink alcohol, perhaps too much. We know this type of gentleman."

"Please," said the young woman, "if you don't let me untie him, I'll run outside and scream for the police."

"I would not advise you, Miss MacNab," said Dr. Hood seriously, "to be in any hurry to get the police. Father Brown, please control these people of yours from your church. Well, we know a little something about Mr. Glass. But what do we know about Mr. Todhunter? Only three things: that he knows how to save money, that he is more or less rich, and that he has a secret. These seem to me to be the three marks of someone who is being blackmailed. Someone (Mr. Glass, obviously) wants his money and has threatened Mr. Todhunter in order to force him to part with his wealth. Mr. Glass, with his faded finery and bad habits and shrill irritated voice, is the kind of man who blackmails. Here we have two men, the very picture of a tragedy. One, a very respectable man with a mystery, and the other, a villain with a nose for mystery. These two men have fought here today, using their fists and some other blunt weapon."

"Are you going to take those ropes off?" asked the young girl, stubbornly.

Dr. Hood put the silk hat carefully on the side table, and went across to the captive. He studied him intently, moving a little bit this way and that, but he answered:

"No, I think these ropes will do very well until the police come and bring handcuffs."

131

CHAPTER SIX
Dr. Hood Solves the Crime

*F*ather Brown, who had been looking at the patterns on the carpet, lifted his round face and said, "What do you mean?"

The man of science had picked up a little dagger from the carpet and was examining it closely as he answered:

"Because you find Mr. Todhunter tied up," he said, "you all jump to the conclusion that Mr. Glass had tied him up; and then, I suppose, escaped. There are four objections to this. First, why would a man so concerned about his clothes leave his hat behind? Second," he continued, moving toward the window, "this is the only exit, and it is locked on the inside. Third, this dagger has a tiny touch of blood on the point, and there is no wound on Mr. Todhunter. Mr. Glass must have the wound on him. All this, I add to the problem of the blackmail. It is much more likely that Mr. Todhunter would have tried to kill the man who was threatening him, rather than Mr. Glass try to kill the person he is hoping to get a steady supply of money from. That would be like killing the goose that laid the golden eggs. That, I think, is the complete story."

"But the ropes?" asked the priest, whose eyes had remained open with absent-minded admiration.

"Ah, the ropes," said the expert, "Miss MacNab wants very much to know why I did not set Mr.

Todhunter free from his ropes. Well, I will tell her. I did not do it because Mr. Todhunter can set himself free from them any time he chooses."

"What?" cried the audience in different tones of astonishment.

"I have looked at the knots on Mr. Todhunter," said Dr. Hood, quietly. "I happen to know something about knots; they are a huge branch in criminal science. Every one of those knots he made himself and could loosen himself; not one of them would have been made by an enemy really trying to trap him. The whole thing of these ropes is a clever fake to make us think he is the victim of a struggle instead of the wretched Mr. Glass, whose wounded body we may find hidden in the garden, or buried in the sand."

There was a rather depressed silence; the room was darkening, the sea-blown branches of the trees looked leaner and blacker than ever, and they seemed to have come closer to the window than before. One could almost fancy they were sea monsters who had crawled up from the sea to observe the end of this tragedy, even as he, the villain and victim of it, the terrible man in the tall hat, had once crawled up from the sea. For the whole air was dense with the darkness of blackmail—a crime concealing a crime; a black bandage on a blacker wound.

CHAPTER SEVEN
Father Brown Solves the Crime

*T*he face of the little Catholic priest, which was usually still and even a little funny-looking, had suddenly become knotted with a frown. It was not the blank curiosity he had when he first entered the room, but a sort of creative curiosity, which comes when a man has the start of an idea. "Say it again, please," he said in a simple way, "Do you mean that Todhunter can tie himself up all alone, and untie himself all alone?"

"That is what I mean," said the doctor.

"Goodness gracious!" cried Father Brown suddenly, "I wonder if it could possibly be that!"

He shuffled across the room rather like a rabbit, and looked with new curiosity into the partly covered face of the captive. Then he turned his own face toward the group.

"Yes, that's it!" he cried with excitement. "Can't you see it in the man's face? Well, look at his eyes!"

Both the Professor and the girl followed the direction of his glance. And although the broad black scarf completely masked the lower half of Mr. Todhunter's face, they could see something curious about the upper part of it.

"His eyes do look strange," cried the young woman, strongly moved. "You are all beasts, I believe it's hurting him!"

"Not that, I think," said Dr. Hood, "the eyes do have a certain expression. But I would interpret those wrinkles as expressing a slight psychological abnormality—"

"Oh, how ridiculous!" cried Father Brown, "can't you see he's laughing?"

"Laughing!" repeated the doctor, with a jolt, "but what on earth can he be laughing at?"

"Well," replied the priest apologetically, "I think he is laughing at you. And I, too, am going to laugh, now that I know about it."

"Now that you know about what?" asked Hood, in frustration.

"Now that I know," replied the priest, "the profession of Mr. Todhunter."

He shuffled around the room looking at one object after another, staring at things and then bursting out with laughter. The other watched him with open-mouthed frustration. He laughed very much over the hat, still more over the broken glass, and was chuckling with amusement when he reached the sword. Then he turned to the criminologist, who was by now very angry.

CHAPTER EIGHT
The Rabbit in the Hat

"Dr. Hood," he cried enthusiastically, "you are a great poet! You have made a poem out of this story, creating a new world out of it! How much more interesting the story is than the mere facts! Indeed, the mere facts are rather commonplace and comic, by comparison."

"I have no idea what you are talking about," said Dr. Hood with indignation. "my facts are all perfectly visible, though not complete. I may have made a few guesses, created some poetry, as you call it, but only where the exact details were yet to be seen. In the absence of Mr. Glass—"

"That's it, that's it," said the little priest, nodding quite eagerly, "that's the first idea to get fixed; the absence of Mr. Glass. He is so extremely absent. I suppose," he added with some thoughtfulness, "that there was never anybody so absent as Mr. Glass."

"Do you mean he is absent from the town?" demanded the doctor.

"I mean he is absent from everywhere," answered Father Brown. "He is absent from humanity, so to speak."

"Do you seriously mean," said the specialist with a smile, "that there is no such person?"

The priest nodded. "It is a pity."

Orion Hood gave a laugh. "Well," he said, "before

we go on to look at the evidence, let us consider what we found here when we first entered this room. If there is no Mr. Glass, whose hat is this?"

"It is Mr. Todhunter's," replied Father Brown.

"But it doesn't fit him," cried Hood impatiently, "He couldn't possibly wear it!"

Father Brown shook his head, "I never said he could wear it," he answered. "I only said it was his hat. Or, if you insist on a shade of difference, a hat that is his."

"And what is the shade of difference?" asked the famous criminologist, a little impatiently.

"My good sir," cried the mild little man, with his first sign of impatience, "if you walked down the street, and went into the nearest hat shop, you would see there is, in common speech, a difference between a man's hat, and hats that are his."

"But the hat shop owner," protested Hood, "would make money selling his new hats. What could Todhunter get out of having an old hat?"

"Rabbits," replied Father Brown promptly.

"*What?*" cried Dr. Hood.

"Rabbits, ribbons, goldfish, rolls of colored paper," said our priest quickly. "Didn't you figure it all out when you saw that the ropes were faked? It's just the same with the sword. Mr. Todhunter hasn't got a scratch on him, as the saying goes; but he's got a scratch inside him, if you understand anything that I am saying."

"Do you mean under his clothes he has a scratch?" asked Mrs. MacNab seriously.

"I do not mean that," said Father Brown. "I mean inside Mr. Todhunter."

"Well, what in the world *do* you mean?" shouted the doctor.

"Mr. Todhunter," explained Father Brown easily, "is learning to be a professional magician, as well as a juggler, ventriloquist,[2] and expert at rope tricks. The conjuring trick explains the hat. The hat has no trace of hair, not because the bald man, Mr. Glass, does not wear it but because no one has ever worn it. The juggling explains the three glasses, which Todhunter was teaching himself to throw up in the air and catch one by one. But, because he is only a beginner at this, he smashed one glass against the ceiling. And the juggling also explains the sword, which Mr. Todhunter was trying to teach himself to swallow for his act. But again, being just a beginner, he must have very slightly nicked the inside of his throat with this weapon. So you see, he has a wound inside him, which I am sure, from the expression on his face, is not very serious at all. He was also practicing the magic trick where someone ties him up, and he must get free of the knots by a certain time, like Houdini in the chained trunk, and he was just about to free himself when we all burst in on his room. The cards, of course, are for card tricks, and they are all over the floor, because he was practicing one of those tricks where you try to send the cards flying through the air from one hand to the other. He only kept his profession a secret because he had to keep his tricks a secret, like any other magician. The mere fact of one snooping man with a top hat at the back window, who was told to get out with a bit of anger in the voice, was enough to set us all on the wrong path, and make us imagine that his whole life was threatened by the dark figure of Mr. Glass."

"But what about the two voices?" asked Maggie, staring in disbelief.

"Have you ever heard a ventriloquist?" asked Father Brown. "Don't you know they speak first in their natural voice, and then answer themselves in just that shrill, squeaky voice that you heard?"

There was a long silence, and Dr. Hood stood looking at the little man who had finished speaking. "You are certainly a very clever person," he said; "you could not have found it done better in a book. But there is still one part of Mr. Glass that you have not explained away successfully, and that is his name. Miss MacNab certainly heard Mr. Todhunter speaking to someone called Mr. Glass."

Father Brown broke into a little giggle. "Well, that," he said, "that's the silliest part of the whole silly story. When our juggling friend here threw up the three glasses one by one, he counted them out loud as he caught them, and was also talking out loud when he failed to catch one. What he really said was 'One, two, three—missed a glass; one, two—missed a glass.' And so on."

There was a second of quiet in the room, and then every one suddenly burst out laughing. As they laughed, the man in the corner freed himself of his ropes. Then he presented himself in the center of the room and bowed. From his pocket he took out a piece of paper, printed in blue and red, which announced that ZALADIN, the World's Greatest Magician,

Juggler, Ventriloquist, and Sword Swallower, would be ready with an entirely new series of Tricks at the Empire Pavilion, in Scarborough, next Monday night, at 8:00 precisely.

Footnotes

1 Criminologist - a person who scientifically studies crimes and/or criminals.

2 Ventriloquist - a professional entertainer who can speak so that his voice seems to come from some other person or place, usually from a dummy which he controls.

www.ingramcontent.com/pod-product-compliance
Lightning Source LLC
Chambersburg PA
CBHW060230180626
46813CB00007B/3035